"Was that too much?" His lips brushed her ear.

She felt the tickle of his mouth against her skin across every inch of her body. Her stomach tightened as she sucked in a breath.

She shook her head. His words were not too much. In fact, she wanted to hear more. Wanted to feel and experience more.

Wesley kissed the outer shell of her ear. "Should I stop and wait for a more appropriate time and place?"

The good, responsible person she'd tried to be for years would say yes. She was still technically at work. Her door wasn't locked. Anyone could come by the office and see her. See them.

Except she didn't have any appointments. No one just dropped in on her at work. All of her appointments were done for the day. The chances of anyone catching them was slim, but the idea of being caught, of the riskiness of it all, made her pulse pound in her ears. She hadn't done anything daring and remotely sexy in so long, she knew she would regret sending him away for the rest of her life.

Dear Reader,

If you've read the first Heart & Soul book, *Summoning Up Love*, then you are familiar with the Livingston brothers. They're hardworking, dedicated to helping people, enthusiastic about paranormal investigations and loyal to each other. While writing *The Spirit of Second Chances*, I wondered which of the brothers would struggle with their newfound success.

Dion is now happily settled with Vanessa, and Tyrone always wanted success, but middle brother Wesley is struggling with the big changes. He's figuring out how to start over, and when the woman who broke his teenage heart asks for help with an investigation, he doesn't view their reconnection as an opportunity for a second chance. Cierra is putting her life back together after a failed marriage and is afraid to put her trust in Wesley after he inadvertently betrayed her trust when they were younger.

I hope you enjoy reading about Wesley and Cierra discovering their new place in life and get all the feels as they get into the spirit of a second chance.

Happy reading,

Synithia

The Spirit of
Second Chances

———

SYNITHIA WILLIAMS

HARLEQUIN

**SPECIAL
EDITION**

HARLEQUIN®
SPECIAL
EDITION™

Recycling programs for this product may not exist in your area.

ISBN-13: 978-1-335-72416-8

The Spirit of Second Chances

For questions and comments about the quality of this book, please contact us at CustomerService@Harlequin.com.

Harlequin Enterprises ULC
22 Adelaide St. West, 41st Floor
Toronto, Ontario M5H 4E3, Canada
www.Harlequin.com

Printed in U.S.A.

Synithia Williams has been an avid romance-novel lover since picking up her first at the age of thirteen. It was only natural that she would begin penning her own romances soon after—much to the chagrin of her high school math teachers. She's a native of South Carolina and now writes romances as hot as their Southern settings. Outside of writing she works on water quality and sustainability issues for local government. She's married to her own personal hero, and they have two sons, who've convinced her that professional wrestling and superheroes are supreme entertainment. When she isn't working, writing, or being a wife and mother, she's usually bingeing on TV series, playing around on social media or planning her next girls' night out with friends. You can learn more about Synithia by visiting her website, www.synithiawilliams.com.

Books by Synithia Williams

Harlequin Special Edition

Heart & Souls

Summoning Up Love

HQN

Jackson Falls

The Promise of a Kiss
Forbidden Promises
Scandalous Secrets
Careless Whispers
Foolish Hearts

Visit the Author Profile page
at Harlequin.com for more titles.

Writing a book can feel lonely and isolating at times, but when I look up from my laptop, I recognize the wonderful support system helping me. My husband and kids, who've accepted my writing career and cheer me on. My writing friends Yasmin, Cheris, Jamie, Dren, Kwana and KD, who gush over covers and help me with plot holes. The people who offer insight on the careers I'm writing about such as Realtor Shondia Lowery Stroman. You all play a part in making this dream a reality. Thank you!

Chapter One

Wesley swore as the Weed Eater jerked in his hands. The loud whirring of the machine switched to a low buzz as the string tangled in the spool. Again. He hit the head of the machine on the ground several times, but that didn't help. With a frustrated sigh he turned it off and tossed the cursed lawn tool to the ground.

If his older brother, Dion, were there, he'd lecture Wesley about not properly handling the equipment. Wesley's younger brother, Tyrone, would point out the multiple weeds he'd missed along the border of their family home. That is, if they were there to help him. Instead, Dion left Sunshine Beach to start a new life in Charlotte with his girlfriend, Vanessa, and Tyrone decided to spend the time before the series premiere of their new ghost investigation show promoting the series. Translation: partying and enjoying the perks of being a soon-to-be celebrity.

Which left Wesley to handle the yard work at the home the three of them shared after their parents died. Dion typically took care of the yard work.

Wesley wasn't good at landscaping. That's why he lived in a condominium and paid fees to cover building and grounds maintenance. If his brothers asked him to keep the inside of the house clean or bake a cake, he could handle that. Except a discussion of the house and the maintenance hadn't happened before Dion and Tyrone left town without a backward glance. As usual, his brothers assumed Wesley would keep things going.

Leaving the uncooperative Weed Eater where he'd thrown it, Wesley walked over to the front porch. The late-afternoon sun filtered through the leaves of the large oak tree that shaded the front of the house. The shade didn't do much to combat the humidity that clung to him like a wet blanket. He grabbed the insulated water bottle he'd left on the porch, opened it and took a long sip of the cool water.

"Hey, Wesley, is that you?" a male voice called from the road.

Wesley looked over at the tall, slim Black man crossing the lawn toward him. He frowned for a second before recognition dawned.

"Calvin?" Wesley said, grinning.

Calvin patted his chest. "The one and only."

Wesley shook his head and met Calvin halfway. Grinning, he slapped hands with Calvin before giving him a quick one-armed hug. "Good ole Calvin. Where you been, man?"

Calvin leaned back and rubbed the back of his head. "I'm still living in DC."

Calvin Kennerly and his family had lived in the house across the street from Wesley and his family since they were kids. They'd grown up together, played together and graduated high school together. After high school, Calvin left to attend Howard University while Wesley opted for Clemson. They saw each other occasionally when Calvin came home to visit, but after he'd got married and had kids, the trips back to Sunshine Beach had dwindled.

"What are you doing in town? Your mom okay?" Concern filled Wesley's voice. He hadn't seen Mrs. Kennerly often in the months since her husband passed away. Typically, she'd be outside working in her garden or sitting on the front porch waving at people passing by. He'd assumed it was because of her grief, and he hoped it wasn't due to declining health.

Calvin nodded. "Yeah, she's good. I finally convinced her to move to DC with me and the family. Now that Dad's gone, the house is too much for her to handle on her own. Plus, I'd like to keep an eye on her now that she's getting older."

"I understand that. She agreed?"

"Yeah. It was hard to convince her to sell the place, but she's ready to start new memories. Or at least that's what she said."

Wesley looked across the street at the two-story

colonial he'd spent almost as many days playing in as his own home. "Dang, you're selling the house. It'll be hard to imagine another family over there."

"There'll be a new family over there before you know it. We didn't realize how quickly the house would sell. The Realtor didn't get the chance to put the sign in the yard before we got offers. Way above our asking price."

Wesley's gaze snapped back to Calvin. "Seriously?"

"Yeah. That's at least one good thing. People are moving to the area and the housing market is fierce. That worked in our favor."

"I'm happy for y'all, but I'm going to hate to see Mrs. Kennerly go. Seems like everything is changing."

First his brothers leaving and now Mrs. Kennerly. He knew the two situations were different and not related, but the heavy feeling of being left behind pressed down on him.

"Oh yeah," Calvin said, snapping his fingers. "I heard about you and your brothers getting that show. Congratulations, man."

Heat prickled Wesley's cheeks as he nodded. Would he ever get used to people congratulating him? He was excited about their new show. He'd wanted it almost as much as Tyrone had, but the attention was hard to adjust to. Wesley wasn't used to being the focus of attention. Dion and Tyrone were the ones people gravitated to and praised. But, again, Dion and Tyrone weren't in town, which meant Wesley had to graciously accept the well-wishes and pretend as if some of the same people had never thought of him as anything other than "the other Livingston brother" beforehand.

"Thanks. It's a blessing and a dream come true," Wesley said in the I'm-grateful-but-not-arrogant tone he'd perfected since the show's announcement. "Who would've thought?"

"I'm not surprised. You and your brothers were always telling those ghost stories you heard from your grandmother and trying to get the rest of us neighborhood kids to check out haunted houses with y'all." Calvin laughed and looked toward the house. "I'm proud of y'all. Are Dion and Tyrone here, too?"

"Nah, Dion moved to Charlotte with his girl and Tyrone is handling some of the promo between filming."

Calvin looked toward the abandoned lawn mower and Weed Eater near the side of the house then back at Wesley. "And they left you here with all the work, huh," he said with a good-natured laugh.

Wesley joined in the laughter, even though he didn't find the situation the least bit humorous. He was happy Dion had finally realized he had options outside of Sunshine Beach and chose to pursue them. He wasn't thrilled with Dion tossing him the keys to the house and assuming Wesley would take care of things. Tyrone's quick departure wasn't as surprising. His younger brother had dreamed of leaving Sunshine Beach for years. The moment Dion left, Tyrone had taken every opportunity to do something related to the show under the guise of promotions. No thought of asking Wesley if he wanted or needed help with keeping the house up now that Dion had moved.

"It's all good," Wesley said this time in his even, everything-is-fine-with-me-and-my-brothers tone.

He would never give anyone a hint of a rift between him and his brothers. When they were teens, "well-meaning" neighbors and extended family members used any disagreement between the brothers as a sign that nineteen-year-old Dion couldn't handle the responsibility of taking care of Wes and Tyrone after their parents died. The rifts had been plenty as the three learned to create a new life together, but Wesley had made a point of smoothing things out quickly and hiding any strife.

He'd fought to avoid them being separated after they lost their parents. At times they'd come close to splitting up. Wesley vividly remembered the times in the first year after their parents died when Dion and Tyrone butted heads and would have got into full-fledged fistfights if Wesley hadn't intervened. But they hadn't split. They'd stuck it out and vowed to be there for each other.

Vows were made to be broken. Wesley chased

away the depressing thought as Calvin continued talking.

"You know, with everything changing in town," Calvin said, "you could easily sell this house. I know you all stayed in it after your parents passed, but now that you're about to be TV stars, you can let the house go and move on to bigger and better things."

Wesley waved off Calvin's words. "Nah, we couldn't sell the house. Not now at least. So tell me, how's the family? You had another kid, right?"

Wesley and Calvin talked for another twenty minutes. They exchanged numbers before Calvin left and Wesley put the lawn equipment in the shed in the back of the house. He went inside, washed his hands and face, and grabbed a beer out of the fridge. It was the last one there from a twelve-pack he and his brothers purchased when they'd last been together after filming their first episode. They'd toasted the show, their lives changing, how they'd always stick together.

Wesley's phone chimed. He opened the group text from his brothers to find a picture of Tyrone on a beach grinning. Dion replied first.

Where you at now?

Miami, Tyrone texted back. Came down for a party.

Miami? What was Tyrone doing in Miami? He'd

said he couldn't come help with the yard this week-end because of some promo event and he'd be back in town the following weekend. Wesley quickly typed out a reply. You coming back this weekend?

Three bubbles hovered on the screen. Wesley raised a brow and waited. A few seconds later Ty-rone replied. Gonna try. Working some new angles to promote the show.

Translation: Tyrone was looking for the next party. Wesley sighed and shook his head. Tyrone had agreed to help him find a contractor to replace the shingles that had fallen off the roof during the last storm. Dion couldn't do it because he had some event at his new job. Wesley would bet his last pay-check Tyrone wasn't showing up.

He closed the text message and opened the inter-net browser. A quick search revealed the value of the houses in the area. His eyes bulged as he looked at the prices the homes in the neighborhood sold for. He didn't need the money, not just because of the show but also because his work as a freelance archi-tect kept him comfortable, but if they sold the house, they could use the profit to purchase more equip-ment and reinvest in their investigation business.

He dropped the phone and shook his head. Nah, he couldn't really sell the house. His brothers wouldn't go for it. He glanced back at the phone. The last house he'd looked at mocked him from the screen. Would talking to a Realtor and getting an idea of the value of their home really hurt? Maybe his brothers would be more open to sell once they saw the benefits.

"It's not like they're going to be around or care about the house," he muttered to himself.

The more he thought of it the more the idea took root and spread. His brothers had moved on with their lives. He was the one left behind, and as usual, his brothers were oblivious to anything Wesley wanted. They assumed he'd be okay with their choices because he typically went along with their decisions. Not this time. This time he'd work his negotiation magic and convince his brothers to do what he wanted for once.

Cierra stared at her mother sitting across from her at the table in her parents' large kitchen. The sound of her five-year-old daughter, Aria, singing along to the Kidz Bop version of BTS's "Dynamite" with Cierra's younger sister, Cetris, in the adjoining living room made her think she'd misheard what her mother had just casually announced.

She glanced from her mother to her father, who leaned casually against the square oak dinette table, back to her mother. Both appeared unfazed by the news they'd dropped in her lap.

"You're joking," she said, disbelief thick in her voice.

Her mom, Olivia, shook her head. "We are not

joking," she said with slight amusement. She slowly brushed aside a lock of silver hair from her face. Her hair, completely gray, fell in loose curls around her face in a way Cierra hoped her hair would mimic when she got up the nerve to stop dying the sporadic grays springing up in her head.

The laugh lines that creased her mom's mahogany skin deepened as she smiled. "You know we don't joke about money."

Cierra's head swung toward her dad. He'd just returned home from golfing with his other retired buddies and wore a dark green polo shirt, which complemented the honey gold of his skin, and tan shorts that were miraculously still creased. His light brown eyes sparkled with the smug I'm-the-world's-best-dad look he got whenever he presented good news, which meant Benjamin Greene was not playing a joke on his oldest daughter.

"They really want me to sell the DeWalt Manor?" Cierra's voice rose with skepticism.

Her parents exchanged an amused look and laughed. Cierra placed her hands over her rapidly beating heart. Excitement coursed through her as the truth of their words sunk in.

"They're really selling the place?" Cierra asked.

Olivia chuckled and nodded. "Apparently, the family has been trying to sell the place for a few years, but no one's agreed to take it off their hands. Your dad played golf with Carolyn DeWalt last week, mentioned you were a Realtor and voilà." Oliva said the words as if that was all it took for the owner of an expensive estate to give Cierra, recently divorced with a real estate firm that was barely in the black, the responsibility of selling their two-hundred-plus-year-old manor.

Cierra narrowed her eyes at her dad. "How did you convince her?"

"I told her the truth," Benjamin said. "You were the top agent at Huger Realty three years in a row. Everyone around here recognizes the name and knows that's one of the best firms in the entire region."

Cierra closed her eyes and took a long breath. She knew the offer was too good to be true. She opened her eyes and tried to hide her disappointment when she spoke. "I was top agent four years ago. Did you tell them I left and started my own firm?"

Her dad waved a hand. "I mentioned that but focused on how good you were there. Why are you worrying? It's not like you left your skills with you when you started your own."

No, she hadn't left her skills, but she'd left behind her support system. She'd left in a rush after discovering her then husband, current ex, had gone behind her back to buy out the previous owners of Huger Realty. Draining most of their savings, putting their home up for collateral and not once mentioning his plans to Cierra until the day it was announced to the rest of the agents. That was the final clip in the thin string tying her to a let's-be-a-good-wife-and-make-this-work-for-Aria mentality.

"And she still agreed to let me sell it knowing I'm not with Huger anymore?" she asked.

"Not only that, but Carolyn agreed to double your commission if you can sell the place within six months," her dad said in a but-wait-there's-more tone often heard at the end of infomercials.

Cierra lifted her chin, warning bells ringing in her head. "Hold up, why would she do that? That house, that land, is worth millions and she's going to just give it to me to sell? What's the catch?"

Her dad glanced at her mom. Cierra turned to her mother, who pursed her lips. "Well, there is a small caveat."

"What small caveat?"

"Supposedly...the house is possessed," her mom said in a rush.

Her dad nodded. "Not possessed. Just haunted. The previous Realtors were all spooked and ran off. Not to mention any potential buyers."

"Wait, so you want me to sell a haunted mansion?" She knew this offer was too good to be true. Rumors swirled all of Cierra's life that the DeWalt Manor was haunted. The DeWalt family was a staple in the county since the late 1800s. Starting in the 1960s, the family could no longer afford to maintain the house and had tried reinventing it, first as a bed-and-breakfast, then as a venue for weddings and other events, but despite their efforts nothing stuck for long.

"We want you to sell a lucrative piece of property and finally turn that firm you insisted on starting into something successful," her mom said.

"I insisted on starting it because I couldn't work with Troy anymore."

Her mom held up a hand. "Let's not go through the reasons you threw away your marriage and career. We've been over that enough. Let's focus on the good news. Your dad got you the biggest client you've had since opening. This is a good thing."

Cierra bit the corner of her bottom lip to stop herself from lashing out. Her parents hadn't agreed with her decision to divorce Troy. They'd claimed to understand her hurt but didn't think it was worth ending her marriage over. She'd tried to explain. Troy's betrayal had been the last straw. The one big lie after catching him in hundreds of other little lies over the ten years of their marriage. Their daughter had been two at the time and even Cierra had wondered if she was making the right decision, but after being free of Troy and his manipulation, she'd struggle to get back on her feet for another ten years before crawling back to him.

Her sister, Cetris, came into the kitchen. The Kidz Bop song had changed to something new, and Aria continued to sing. A sheen of sweat covered

Cetris's brown skin and she fanned herself as she walked to the kitchen.

"I'm going to lose ten pounds dancing with Aria," she said laughing. Many people said Cierra and Cetris looked alike, but after ten years of marriage and a kid, Cierra no longer saw the resemblance. Cetris, with her short, natural hair that brought out the cuteness of her heart-shaped face and an unbothered attitude that came from not spending a decade in a bad marriage, had a glow Cierra envied.

Her sister's interruption kept Cierra from going into the defensive mode she'd almost fell into after her mom's throw-away-your-marriage comment. "If she isn't drawing, she'll dance and sing all day," Cierra said.

"I'm about to get the coloring book and have her make me a new masterpiece." Cetris pulled a bottle of water from the fridge and opened it. "What are y'all talking about?"

"Mom and Dad worked it out so I can be the Realtor for the DeWalt Manor."

Cetris spit out the water she'd sipped. Her mom scowled and she gave an apologetic smile as she wiped her mouth. The smile only lasted a second before her head cocked to the side. "Wasn't that place a plantation back in the day?"

"It's not a plantation now," her dad said.

"And it's worth millions, and Cierra could use the commission on that," her mom added on for effect.

Cetris held up her hand in surrender. "All right, I'm just saying. It was a plantation."

Cierra was well aware of the place's history. She'd had to struggle through an "old South" tour of the place back in middle school. Even then she'd barely stopped herself from rolling her eyes over the life-wasn't-that-bad spin the tour guide had put on the place. She hadn't visited the manor since that school trip and honestly hadn't thought much about the place at all. That didn't mean she was unaware of how much the home and land were worth. She *was* a Realtor.

"I don't care what the place used to be," Cierra said. "I need the money."

Selling the manor was just what her struggling firm needed. The property and the surrounding lands had both river and beach access. If she could sell it, for twice the commission no less, she could finally attract other real estate agents to work for her and turning a profit wouldn't completely rely on her. She wouldn't feel like was struggling to prove herself after the loads of criticism she'd received when she'd been accused of leaving Troy for nothing.

"Hey, you know I'm about getting your money," Cetris said.

Cierra sighed and put her head in her hand. "But how am I supposed to sell a haunted mansion?"

"Ooh, ooh, ooh," Cetris said, bouncing on her feet. Cierra and her parents both looked at her expectantly. "The Livingston brothers."

Cierra frowned. "Who?"

"You remember, Wesley, Dion and Tyrone Livingston. I know you don't live in Sunshine Beach anymore, but you have to have heard that they investigate ghosts."

"I didn't know that." The truth was she made a point to not know anything about Wesley Livingston since she'd moved from the town of Sunshine Beach and farther inland toward Georgetown.

Cetris must have noticed the look on her face. She shook her head and came over to the table. She pointed one gray painted nail at Cierra. "Stop it. I don't care about how you feel about what happened in high school."

Her mom leaned forward, and her dad frowned. "What happened in high school?" they asked simultaneously.

"Nothing," Cierra and Cetris replied at the same time. Her parents exchanged a look, but Cetris kept talking.

"If you want to sell this place and need to know why it's haunted, he can help. So figure out what's more important—your teenage pride or your adult pockets."

Cierra didn't need to think about it. Her adult pockets. To get her company out of the red, she was more than willing to reach out to the first guy to break her heart.

Chapter Two

Wesley had finally settled down in the back corner of Cool Beans, a coffee shop in downtown Sunshine Beach, when someone tapped his shoulder. He closed his eyes and cringed. All he'd wanted was a few minutes of quiet after spending the day drafting the layout for a new hotel for one of his clients. He loved working on building designs and typically enjoyed getting lost in a new project. Today, though, his phone had rung nonstop. Calls from their manager and publicist to set up interviews and promotions for their show's premiere were also interrupted by calls from old "friends" and cousins he hadn't seen since the family reunion before his parents passed away.

Everyone wanted a piece of him and his brothers. While he didn't regret their decision to do a reality show following them on ghost investigations, he hadn't truly anticipated how much his life would change. Yes, they were on television, but it wasn't as if they were heading the most anticipated new drama to debut on Netflix. He'd expected a small cult following, not for everyone in their town to treat him and his brothers like A-list stars.

The tap on his shoulder came again. "Excuse me, Wesley?"

The woman's voice was soft and hesitant. Pushing back the irritation of being disturbed, he put down the science fiction book he'd hoped to read while enjoying a banana nut muffin and coffee and turned in his seat.

"Ye…" The word died on his lips. "Cierra?"

Cierra Greene leaned down toward him. Her cocoa-brown eyes widened, and her full lips parted. For a second, he was speechless as the entire English language disappeared from his mind. He hadn't seen Cierra in years, yet she was just as breathtaking as she'd been when they'd been lab partners in high school. He had no idea how he'd passed chemistry back then, because he'd spent most of the class covertly studying everything about Cierra. From the way the sunlight reflected off her rich, dark brown skin, to the way her hair brushed the tops of her shoulders, to her cute cupid's bow of a mouth that seemed to always curl up in a smile.

Crush wasn't an adequate word for what he'd felt for Cierra. Thankfully, he'd played it cool and accepted the superficial friendship she'd bestowed upon him as her chemistry lab partner. While Wesley hadn't been an outcast in high school, his older brother, Dion, student athlete extraordinaire, and his younger brother, Tyrone, the cute playboy everyone loved, were the ones who garnered attention. He'd never expected Cierra to show interest in him romantically, but he'd believed she had. Something he'd realized was a stupid mistake after she'd played him for a fool.

Cierra's lips lifted in a smile that brightened his dark corner of the coffee shop as she straightened. "Oh good, you remember me," she said as if he could possibly forget her.

How could he forget Cierra Greene? Head cheerleader, class president, most popular girl in school and slayer of teenage boy's hearts.

"Yeah... I remember you." He managed to keep his voice calm even though his heart thumped as if he'd had a dozen cappuccinos.

"I was worried because you didn't return any of my calls." She tilted her head to the side and her thick, dark hair shifted. Her smile didn't go away, but there was the barest hint of accusation in her voice.

Wesley shifted in his seat. He hadn't returned her calls because ever since the day Cierra told him after a basketball game that she was ditching him for his former best friend, he'd vowed to never speak to her again. He realized vows made in high school didn't have to follow him into adulthood, but the moment he'd heard her voice message saying she'd like to meet up and talk, he'd deleted it and tried to move on with his life.

"I've been busy," he said.

"Good thing I caught you here then, huh?" She moved to the opposite side of the table and pulled out the other chair and sat.

"How did you know I was here?"

"Mrs. Montgomery," she said as if he should have known that one of the most respected women in town would give his whereabouts to Cierra. She must have read the confusion on his face, because she laughed, that lighthearted laugh that, unfortunately, still made his heart skip a beat. "When I couldn't reach you, my mom called around. Mrs. Montgomery said you typically spend Friday afternoons here. So, here I am!" She held out her arms and spoke as if she were a present.

Her bright smile and enthusiasm stunned him for a second. Wesley cleared his throat and took a sip of his coffee to compose himself. How many years later, fifteen, and he still had the lingering remnants of a crush on her?

Come on, Wes, you gotta do better than that!

He took a long breath and looked back at her. "Here you are."

Her arms lowered slowly, and her smile dimmed. She shifted in her seat before rubbing the back of her neck. He knew that move, too. The nervous tick she used to do when the teacher called on her and she wasn't quite sure of the answer. He hadn't known why she got nervous; she always got the answer right. Cierra Greene had not only been beautiful, but she was also smart and the picture of perfection. When she wasn't crushing hearts.

"Is this a bad time?"

It was a bad time. He came here on Fridays after the lunch rush and before the after-work crowd filled the coffee shop. He could get a perfect, peaceful hour to read and enjoy his favorite muffin before getting into whatever his brothers dragged him into for the night. Except his brothers were no longer in town. Which meant, other than being rude and saying he'd rather read than give her a few minutes, he didn't have a good reason to tell her to leave.

"Nah, I'm good. What's up?"

The uncertainty in her gaze drifted away and she straightened her shoulders. "I was hoping you could help me."

He barely stopped himself from rolling his eyes. Of course she wanted something. Everyone wanted something. "Help you with what?"

"There's this house I'm trying to sell, well, the owners have been trying to sell it for a while, but they can't."

"I'm not looking to buy a house."

She shook her head and laughed. "I don't want you to buy it. I want you to investigate it. The owners say it's haunted or something and that's scared off potential buyers. Now they're desperate to get it off their hands and they've come to me for help."

He'd known she wouldn't reach out to him because she wanted to apologize for dumping him for his best friend back in high school. She'd married the guy and they'd moved one town over to live their perfect life. Still, a wave of disappointment that she'd sought him out after all these years just for a ghost investigation had him glaring into his coffee. "And you're desperate so you came to me?"

The corners of her mouth stiffened. "Not quite. I mean, you do this, right? You hunt ghosts?"

Wesley held up a hand. "I don't hunt ghosts. My brothers and I investigate paranormal activity."

"Either way, you know what to do. Right now, I need someone who knows what to do." She sat up and grinned. "And I know you know exactly what to do."

That smile, her praise, the sparkle in her eye. All three combined to make him sit up straighter and puff out his chest. Two seconds later he realized he was being blinding by the brightness that was Cierra Greene. A sparkling show of enthusiasm and bubbliness that kept him from seeing the truth of her feelings when he was younger. She still knew how to draw someone in. Disgusted with himself for feeling *things* for her knowing her sparkling personality really hid a manipulative heart, he shook his head.

"Sorry, Cierra, but I can't help you."

* * *

Cierra took in Wesley's shaking head and stern eyes and felt as if her world was falling apart. He couldn't help her? If he couldn't help her, then who would? She didn't know anyone else who investigated this type of stuff. She hadn't kept up with Wesley and what he'd done with his life after high school. College, marriage, a career, pregnancy and a messy divorce had kept her out of the business of her old high school classmates. Still, after Cetris recommended Wesley and his brothers, she had to do some digging to believe it.

Wesley was the last person she would have guessed investigated ghosts. Sure, they'd talked about the haunted places around Sunshine Beach, and she knew he'd loved horror and fantasy novels, but he was also the poster child for the science, technology, engineering and math brigade. She'd assumed he was off somewhere discovering the cure for cancer or building the world's first rocket to Jupiter or something. Instead, he was still in Sunshine Beach—surprisingly—and he investigated ghosts on the side.

"Why can't you help me?" Her voice came out more accusing than she'd intended. "Isn't that what you do?"

"I do." His voice and gaze didn't waver.

She waited for a reason why, but her wait was in vain. "Then why can't you investigate my ghost?"

"Because of my schedule. We're in the middle of preparing for the first season."

She raised a brow. "Season of what?"

"Our television show."

Her jaw dropped. "You've really got a television show?"

He pursed his lips and gave her an are-you-for-real look. "You didn't know?"

"I mean...I heard you and your brothers had a television show, but I didn't really think that's what you'd be doing." Not Wesley of all people. The Wesley she remembered preferred sitting quietly in the corner casually observing or immersed in a book. Wesley was not a person she would have expected to be in television.

"What did you think I'd be doing?"

"I don't know. You were so good in chemistry lab I wondered if you were off inventing things."

He watched her for a few seconds before taking a sip of his coffee. "I work as a freelance architect. The ghost investigations were something I did on the side until my brother Tyrone made a connection that turned into a television show."

He spoke so casually. As if getting a television show wasn't a big deal. Maybe it wasn't for Wesley. He'd always been unbothered, calm and collected. Those were the qualities that had drawn her to him when they were younger.

"That's pretty cool. Where can I watch it?"

"It's not on air, yet. We just finished filming the first season. It's in postproduction and should air this fall."

"Congratulations. I figured you'd go on to do great things and here you are doing just that."

He seemed embarrassed by her praise and glanced away quickly before meeting her eye again. "It all worked out."

She cocked her head to the side and studied him. "If you're finished filming, then why wouldn't you be able to investigate the place I'm trying to sell?"

He blinked. "Huh?"

"You said you couldn't help because of the television show. Well, the show isn't filming right now. Doesn't that mean you should be able to help me?"

"I would, but you know, my brothers aren't in town. Dion moved to Charlotte and Tyrone is out promoting the new show."

She smirked and shook her head. "I don't believe for a second that you're saying you need your brothers to help you. Back in high school you never wanted to be linked with or compared to one of your brothers. You can't tell me that much has changed."

"I wasn't like that."

"Yes you were. We even talked about it in chemistry lab. You said you hated the way everyone always compared you to Dion or Tyrone and I told you that I liked you because of who you were and not because of your brothers."

An awkward silence filled the space after her words. She hadn't realized she remembered all that. After she and Wesley fell out as friends, she'd focused on moving forward with her life and forgetting the talks they'd have in lab, the way his dry sense of humor would make her laugh, and how his mellow personality and logical thinking always made him seem older and infinitely more interesting than the other guys in high school. She'd crushed on him hard, and thought he had a crush on her, too. Only to realize too late that he viewed her as just another classmate he was eager to escape from when he graduated high school.

She never could stand a long awkward silence, so she pressed on. She wasn't someone to take the first no as a final answer. "So will you help me?"

"What?"

She chuckled and lightly slapped his hand resting on the table. "Don't say *what*, just say *yes*. If you're good enough to get a show, then that means you're good enough to help me figure out what's going on at the DeWalt Manor."

He leaned forward. "Hold up. You're selling the DeWalt Manor?"

Finally, he sounded interested. "Sure am. Does that make this more appealing?" She leaned forward and wiggled her brows.

Wesley looked away and sipped his coffee. "When

we asked about investigating the house for the show, they said no."

"Really? I'm surprised since they can't sell it because of the ghosts. I heard they're evil spirits."

"Evil spirits are typically people who have a grudge. Sometimes a legitimate one, and knowing the history of that place, I wouldn't be surprised if that were the case here."

Cierra remembered the rebranding once the De-Walt family decided that holding birthday parties and bridal showers at the "DeWalt Plantation" wasn't a good look.

"I can't promise that you can investigate for the show, but maybe if you help me, they'll be willing to let you film some of your investigation." She wasn't sure if that was the case at all, but she was sure of herself. She'd figure out a way to convince Carolyn DeWalt that if she wanted her family manor gone, she would have to trust Cierra's plan to have Wesley investigate.

His brows drew together as he thought. She reached over and placed her hand on his. "Please, Wesley, I really need to sell this place. If I don't, then I'm not sure if I can keep my business open. I don't usually beg, but right now I'm begging you. Help me find out what's going on."

She held her breath and waited. His hand was warm beneath hers. She had a quick memory of the way she'd hold his hand in chemistry lab as they waited to see if their experiment would come out correctly. How her heart would speed up and her breathing would catch from the simple, innocent touch. Her heart hadn't fluttered in years but as she held on to Wesley not only did her pulse increase but something stirred deep in her midsection.

Wesley pulled on his hand. She let him go immediately, heat filling her face as she prayed he hadn't seen any remnants of that foolish high school crush in her eyes.

"I'll help you," he blurted out.

Relief and happiness chased away the moment of embarrassment. She pushed aside the weird reaction she'd had from touching him and focused on her reason for seeking him out in the first place. She was one step closer to closing the biggest deal of her fledging business. She'd suppress any and all old feelings she had in order to sell the DeWalt Manor.

Smiling, she clasped her hands in front of her chest. No need to tempt fate by touching him again. "Thank you, Wesley. I promise you won't regret this."

Wesley looked as if he already regretted the decision. He lifted his mug and took another sip of his coffee. As his tongue swept across his lower lip and Cierra's stomach clenched, she swallowed a groan. He might regret this, but she really hoped *she* didn't eventually regret bringing Wesley back into her life.

Chapter Three

Cierra parked in the drive along the side of the DeWalt Manor. Wesley's car wasn't there, but she wasn't worried about that. She'd arrived early to take pictures of the front of the house before going inside to meet with Carolyn.

The DeWalt Manor, a white two-story home with black shutters, sat in the middle of a sprawling green yard. A wide covered porch spanned the length of the front, and black rocking chairs swayed lazily in the afternoon breeze. The smell of the river, which meandered through the back of the grounds out to the ocean, drifted on the wind. As she snapped pictures, she thought about the family who'd lived there, the history of the land, the people who'd worked there. So many people had touched this place. She could only imagine the stories of those people hidden within the home's bricks and mortar.

Wesley arrived just as Cierra finished taking pictures of the front of the house. She watched as he got out of his car and walked toward her with a swagger that labeled him as a man sure of himself and his capabilities. The breeze pressed the material of his light gray button-up shirt against his muscled chest and his bicep flexed as he brought a hand to his forehead to protect his eyes from the sun.

Thank goodness for her shades, otherwise he might have caught her moment of weakness as she'd let her gaze travel the long length of his body. She'd like to blame her appreciation of Wesley's good looks and sex appeal on her absence of a sex life since her divorce three years ago, but that wasn't the reason. Back in high school, when she was still figuring out her body's sexual responses, she'd reacted to him.

"Hey, you're here!" she said with much more brightness than she'd planned. The sunny tone was a defense mechanism. Cover up any insecurities with cheerfulness and a "can-do" attitude. Something her parents drilled into her since enrolling her in her first dance class at the age of five.

Wesley walked up to her. He dropped the hand from his face and his eyes narrowed as he stared down at her. She wasn't sure if it was from the sun or her overly cheerful greeting. "I said I'd be here. Did you think I'd back out?"

"I don't know. Would you have agreed if you weren't already interested in investigating this place?" She kept her voice light, but she was curious to know his answer. She knew back in high school Wesley hadn't cared for her as much as she'd once assumed he had, but she'd hoped that as adults they could work together without the awkwardness that plagued their teenage years.

Wesley turned toward the house. "So this is the place."

Cierra pursed her lips but let his lack of an answer slide. Did she really want to hear him say out loud that working with her wasn't something on his most-fun-things-to-do list? Besides, his reason for helping her didn't matter. She needed to sell the manor and he wanted an in for his television show. They were both mutually benefitting from this completely impersonal arrangement.

"It's the place," she said.

He placed his hands on his hips and stared at the house. "Man, I haven't been here since—"

"That field trip in middle school," Cierra finished.

He glanced back at her. "You remember that?"

She nodded. "Yeah, as if a bunch of kids really wanted to visit a plantation as part of a Civil War history lesson."

Wesley shook his head. "I'd hoped we would take an overnight trip to Gettysburg or some other battlefield."

"Really? Why?"

"Why do you think? The ghosts?" he said as if the answer should've been obvious.

She waved a hand and shivered. "Yeah, you can keep that. I prefer to leave ghosts alone."

"Then why take on this property?"

"I need this money."

His eyes widened and Cierra shrugged. She wasn't embarrassed to admit the reason why she'd agreed to sell the house because she wasn't embarrassed about doing what it took to make her own brokerage successful. Being bashful about going after her goals wasn't in her nature. Not when she'd grown up in a household where anything less than your best wasn't acceptable.

"Is Troy not working?"

Cierra looked away. "Oh, he's working. Troy and I divorced three years ago. It wasn't pretty and it's part of the reason why I need to sell this property to make my real estate business profitable." She pointed toward the house. "Let's go in."

She walked toward the house before Wesley could say anything. She didn't want to see his reaction to hearing about her divorce. Wesley and Troy had once been good friends. Troy was the one who'd helped Cierra realize her romantic feelings toward Wesley were in vain. After she and Troy started dating, his friendship with Wesley slowly faded away until they were no longer speaking to each other by the time Troy and Cierra married after college.

Wesley followed her lead and said nothing as they walked up the stairs and rang the bell. Maybe he didn't want to relive the old days and a long-lost friendship any more than she wanted to go into the reasons why she and Troy hadn't worked out.

A white woman dressed in a pink gingham sheath dress answered the door. Her reddish-brown hair hung in waves to her shoulders and a welcoming smile brought out dimples in her round cheeks. "You must be Cierra," she said.

Cierra nodded. "I am, and you're Carolyn De-Walt?"

Carolyn pressed a hand to her chest. "That's me."

"It's nice to meet you, Carolyn." Cierra pointed to Wesley next to her. "This is Wesley Livingston. He's going to help me figure out what's going on so we can get your place sold."

Relief filled Carolyn's eyes. "That would be a relief." She stepped back so they could enter the spacious foyer. "Wesley, I believe your brother contacted my husband about doing an investigation here, am I right?"

"My brother Tyrone. We were filming our paranormal investigation show at the time and thought this place would be a good location."

Carolyn toyed with her pearl earring and glanced around the room. "My husband was afraid that if we invited a show here to investigate, it would scare off prospective buyers." Carolyn shook her head. "We don't want to scare people off."

Carolyn led them from the foyer into one of the front rooms. Cierra's foggy memory from the middle school trip kicked in and she thought the room with the pale green walls and antique furnishings was a parlor.

Cierra gave her a confident smile. "We'll get to the bottom of things and have your property on the market and sold to a new buyer before you know it."

Carolyn nodded quickly. "That would be good."

"Why are you selling?" Wesley asked. "This property has been in your family for generations."

Carolyn raised a shoulder. "It's becoming too much to take care of. Over the years we've tried different ways to make money off the place. A bed-and-breakfast, event venue and old South tours but…strange things would happen and guests would warn others away. I'm the last remaining family member with control over the property and I'd like to be rid of it. When your dad mentioned how good you are at selling properties, I decided to try again."

Wesley spoke up again. "Is there anything in the house's history that could give us a place to start?"

Carolyn vigorously shook her head. "No, nothing in the house or on the property. The history is good."

Cierra raised a brow. "All the way back to when the house was built?" Considering the age of the home, and its origins, she couldn't imagine the history being completely spotless.

"I know what you're thinking," Carolyn said, straightening her shoulders. "The place started as a…plantation…but the family records from that time show that the family treated all of the…people here well. My fourth great-grandmother even freed everyone before the war ended."

Cierra and Wesley exchanged a look before Wesley rubbed his chin and cleared his throat. For a moment Cierra considered letting the statement pass. She needed this sale and alienating her client wasn't the way to do that, but she couldn't hold back.

"That may be, but living a life knowing you're considered property comes with a pain none of us will ever understand. I get that your family may have tried to be better than others, but that doesn't mean the spirits of those who died here don't have more to say."

Carolyn's cheeks reddened. "You're right. I'm sorry. I just don't know what's going on or what to do. Your dad convinced me that you could sell this place and that's all I want. I no longer want that part of my family history to be my legacy. I just want to get rid of this house and if you can do that, then that's all I ask for."

An hour later, Wesley stood on the brick patio at the back of the manor overlooking the river in the distance. Carolyn had left thirty minutes earlier after saying she had somewhere else to be and giving them permission to explore the home and grounds to prepare for the sale. It hadn't escaped

Wesley that she'd suddenly had an appointment around the same time he'd felt the tingling presence of a spirit in the room. As soon as he'd felt the cool brush across his skin, Carolyn's eyes widened, and she'd started stuttering. She'd practically run from the house in her rush. He guessed she could sense the presence as well.

"What do you think?" Cierra asked him as they stood in the shade.

"I think there's something going on here."

Her eyes widened. "Really? You can tell that already?"

He nodded. "My brothers always say I'm more in tune with what's happening than they are. There is definitely a presence here, but I didn't feel anger or evil intentions."

"What did you feel?"

She watched him with curiosity and no judgment. The tension in his shoulders eased. He never knew how people would react when he talked about investigations or the way he quickly sensed if there was a presence in a space along with the emotions of those left behind.

"I felt a sense of curiosity and interest. It grew even more after Carolyn left, but there was something else. I don't know what it is, but I think there's more to this house and its history than we know." He looked back at the house. The familiar excitement of uncovering the secrets within bubbled up in his system.

"Do you think she's keeping something from us?"

"I don't know. She may not know all the history. Family secrets aren't always passed down. Especially the bad ones."

Cierra sighed. "Isn't that the truth."

"I could only imagine the secrets my family home has. We weren't the first family to live there, and I've always wondered what the people who lived there before were like."

"Have you ever felt anything there?"

"Nah, that's the one place where I've never felt a presence."

"Do you want to feel a presence?"

Every time he entered his family home a small part of him hoped to feel the warmth and affection of his parents. Some sign that a part of them stuck around to watch over them, but he never did. He supposed he should be happy they weren't lingering with unfinished business, but the kid in him still yearned for another moment with his parents.

"Sometimes I do," he admitted. "But I won't have to worry about that soon. Not after I sell the place."

Her lips parted with her quick inhale. "You're selling the house?"

"I think so. I haven't put it on the market, yet, and I need to convince my brothers, but with all the changes in our life I don't think we need to hold on to the house anymore."

She stepped closer to him. "Who's your Realtor?"

Her nearness, and the smile hovering on her full lips, distracted him for a second. "No one. It's still early."

She grabbed his hand. "Let me sell it."

"What?" His gaze darted from the excited gleam in her eyes to where her soft hand clasped his.

"Let me be your Realtor. You're helping me here, let me help you, too. Since I'm getting double the commission here I'll cut my fee in half for you. I can come by tomorrow or later this week to take a look and give you some suggestions of what to do before you sell."

He pulled on his hand. He didn't like the way the warmth from her touch seemed to spread up his arm and toward his chest. "I don't know about that."

She held on tight. "Why not? You just said you want to sell. Let me give you an idea of what you can get for the house. We can help each other out. Okay?"

She wiggled his hand and bounced on her feet. She was close enough for her bubbly energy to send an electric charge across his skin. She smiled up at him as if he were the answer to her problems and before his brain could register what was going on he nodded.

Cierra's smile went from cute to radiant and she

squeezed his hand. "Good. When do you want me to come by?"

Wesley was a chump. One hand grip and smile and he was agreeing to let her sell the house. He'd just come up with the idea to sell and still needed to get his brothers' buy-in. Selling was for the best considering both Dion and Tyrone had moved on with their lives without a second thought for him. That didn't mean he liked agreeing to Cierra's suggestion just because her nearness, and the tantalizing smell of her perfume, had reminded him of all the reasons why he'd once been smitten with her.

He snatched his hand away and took a step back. "I've got to go. I'll get with you later this week about the investigation." He turned and walked toward the front of the house before he lost even more of his mind and did something stupid like fall for Cierra again.

Chapter Four

Cierra had just finished putting together the comparable sales for her meeting with Wesley that afternoon when the doorbell rang. She glanced up from the dining room table to her daughter lying in the middle of the living room floor surrounded by multiple colored pencils as she traced some of her favorite cartoon characters on the screen of her tablet.

"That's Aunt Cetris," Cierra said in a singsong voice.

Aria's chocolate-brown eyes brightened. A wide smile creased her cute face and revealed her two missing front teeth. "Yay!" She jumped to her feet, the pink and purple beaded necklaces she wore that matched her pink-and-purple jumpsuit swung around her neck as she spun toward the door.

"Wait for me. You know the rule." Cierra stood and crossed the open floorplan to stand next to Aria.

"I know, Mommy, I know." She took Cierra's hand and pulled. "Hurry up and let in Aunt Cetris."

Cierra shook her head and laughed as her daughter dragged her to the door. She checked through the blinds covering the window next to the door and confirmed before opening. Even though she expected Cetris, and her sister texted to say she would be right over, Cierra didn't want to be surprised by her ex-husband on the other side. She'd finally convinced Troy that popping up whenever he felt like it wasn't acceptable, but for a man who still thought that despite the divorce he had some type of claim on her, she wondered how long he'd continue following her wishes.

She opened the door and waved her sister in. "Thank you so much for this."

Cetris strolled in looking effortlessly easy, breezy and beautiful in an off-the-shoulder yellow sundress that was oversize yet still seemed to bring out her curvy figure. Cierra immediately felt like a stuffy old divorced lady in the white top she'd paired with a pair of slim-fitting black slacks and a blue blazer.

"You know it's no problem. I love babysitting my little artist extraordinaire." Cetris bent over and hugged Aria.

Aria wiggled out of Cetris's embrace and jumped up and down. "Come see my pictures!"

"I'm coming. I'm coming." Cetris gave Cierra a wink as Aria pulled her farther into the house.

Cierra packed her items up while Aria showed Cetris all her pictures. She may not be as effortlessly sexy as her younger sister but that was fine. She wasn't going for that. Today's meeting was about making a good impression when she met with Wesley. Not only because she had a feeling he didn't want her to be the one to help sell his house, but because she wanted him to believe in her abilities. Back when she'd considered them friends, Wesley had looked at her with respect and admiration. Everyone had. Back then she'd been viewed as the person most likely to do great things with her life, like become the first woman president or something.

Somewhere between getting married young and working in her husband's shadow, people stopped looking at her as if she were in control and began deferring to Troy. Even though she was the top seller at Huger Realty, Troy always pointed out that they were a husband-and-wife team. At first she swallowed her pride as the admiration for her faded and the accolades went to them together, with Troy typically standing front and center to accept.

They were a team. Her success equaled their success and vice versa. She'd believed that, or at least tried to convince herself of that as more people stopped looking at her as if she had all the answers and viewed her as if she was Troy's secretary. How else would he have been able to purchase the company without anyone thinking to consult her?

She didn't want Wesley to look at her as if she didn't know what she was doing and she didn't want to explore why. She already knew she was not Wesley's type and wasn't about to get lost in a romantic notion that she could rekindle a flame with her high school crush. Things like that only happened in cable TV movies.

"Who's the client today?" Cetris asked after Aria went to her room to grab a different art notebook.

"Wesley Livingston. He's thinking about selling their family home."

Cetris's eyes widened. "For real? I didn't think they'd ever sell. But you know, now that Dion moved to Charlotte and they've got that new TV show, maybe they don't need it anymore."

Cierra shrugged. "I don't know. I was surprised when he mentioned it. They fought hard to keep the house after their parents died, but maybe things have changed."

"You sound like you're not sure if he should sell."

She wasn't sure. She'd been shocked when he mentioned selling the place when she knew how hard he'd worked to keep him and his brothers together in the house. But that was back in high school, and they were older now with different goals. He had a television show and his brothers had moved on. She needed a profitable and visible sell to draw Realtors to her business. What mattered now was making the sale and proving to Wesley she could deliver.

"I'm trying to finally end a year in the black and not the red." She put the last file in her leather book bag then swung it onto her back. "That house will go fast and for a great profit. If he wants to sell, then I'm going to sell it."

Cetris cocked her head to the side. "I can't believe you're working with him. Back in high school you said you'd never talk to him again."

"That was high school and I'm not about to let my hurt feelings stop me from making money."

"But you did have a crush on him. You know, I was just watching this movie about a woman who went home—"

Cierra held up a hand. "Stop! I already know how this story ends because you always make me watch those sappy movies. This is business. That is all. There will be no rekindling of feelings from when I was seventeen. I've been married, had a kid and gone through a messy divorce. Those feelings are long gone."

"But you said you're ready to date again."

"I am, but that doesn't mean I'm going backward. Trying to date Wesley is not only going backward, it's almost like a time travel phenomenon and movies have proven time travel is a bad idea."

Cetris rolled her eyes and laughed. "First of all, time travel isn't bad in every movie. Second, Wesley is kind of a good catch. He's quiet, he's cute and he hasn't been running through every woman in town like his brother Tyrone. You just don't know it because you don't live in Sunshine Beach."

Cierra looked at her watch. "Once again, I'm

ready to date but it will not be the guy who humili-
ated me back in high school. I want to get some, but
I'm far from desperate. Danny the Dildo is working
just fine for now."

Her sister cackled and slapped a hand over her
mouth. "Girl, please stop. I'm gonna need you to
break up with Danny and find a real man."

Cierra would like to find a real man. Danny the
Dildo was useful in a pinch, but it was not the same
as having a warm body pressed against hers. Hands
caressing her skin. Full lips trailing across her neck,
shoulders and breasts.

A vision of Wesley's dark eyes, full lips and wide
shoulders floated into her brain. Cierra shook her
head. Damn Cetris and her putting stupid ideas in
her head.

Aria came running back into the room, thankfully interrupting the conversation and preventing
Cetris from giving her more grief.

Cierra went over and kissed the top of her head.
"Okay, Mommy's going to work now."

Aria grinned and gave her a thumbs-up. "Sell
the house for a lot of money."

Cierra smiled at her daughter's encouragement.
"Mommy's gonna try. Love you. Listen to Aunt
Cetris."

"Yes, ma'am." Aria hugged her again before
dropping to the floor to start drawing again.

Cierra gave Cetris a thumbs-up. "I'll be back in

about two hours or so. I'll call if I'm going to be late."

"Take your time. I'm good with my little artist here. Tell Wesley I said hi." Cetris waved her fingers as she said the word *hi* in a breathy tone.

Cierra shook her head and left. If her sister wanted to drool over Wesley Livingston, then she could. Cierra got it. The man was still as fine as he'd been in high school. Finer if she were being honest. But she meant what she'd said. She was only trying to earn Wesley's respect and admiration. That was it. Her heart and her malnourished libido would just have to get on board with her brain.

Cierra arrived at Wesley's family home and snapped a few pictures of the outside before going to the door. Even though they'd been cool with each other back in high school, she'd never been to his home. She was immediately charmed by the house's curb appeal. The light blue home, with black shutters and white columns, was surrounded by a smooth green lawn, and large shade trees gave the house a welcoming feel. She could easily imagine her and Aria sitting on the front porch sipping tea and waving at neighbors as they passed by, Wesley swaying next to her in one of the rocking chairs as he read the latest fantasy novel.

Cierra shook her head quickly. Nope, no time for happy family fantasies. Especially with Wesley, who barely looked at her as if she were a woman, much less one who would capture his interest. Besides, she'd succumbed to the "happy family" fantasy before and had the divorce papers to prove just how much believing in happily-ever-afters could damage a person. She was on the lookout for a happy-for-now relationship. A part-time companion: that was all.

She rang the bell and Wesley answered the door shortly after. He was dressed casually in a stylish pair of jeans and a light blue T-shirt that stretched across his shoulders and chest. His dark eyes met hers and he appeared neither pleased nor particularly excited about her being there. Typically, clients were excited about selling their house. Maybe he was nervous about entering the housing market. That's what she would go with versus thinking he wished she hadn't shown up.

She lifted a hand and did a quick wave. "Good afternoon! Are you ready to get started?" She filled her voice with the bright enthusiasm that typically got her what she wanted from people.

Wesley blinked and glanced away quickly. "Um... yeah. Come in." He stepped back so she could enter.

Smiling, Cierra crossed the threshold into the house. The smell of something sweet and delicious greeted her. She took a deep breath. "What smells so good?"

"I made cinnamon rolls while I waited," he said.

Cierra stopped in her tracks. She eyed him skeptically. "Really?"

He nodded slowly. "Really."

"You mean the ones from the can?"

He scowled and shook his head. "No, ma'am. When I bake, it's from scratch. Get it right."

She raised her brows and eyed him in a new light. He sounded affronted at the thought of making them from a can. Which meant she now had to try them herself. "Well, I love cinnamon rolls."

Wesley's eyes narrowed. She just continued to smile and wait. He couldn't just throw that out there and not offer her any. The corner of his mouth lifted in a half smile and he let out a soft laugh.

"Come get one," he said and headed farther into the house.

Cierra did a fist pump and followed. The interior of the house was clean but dated. The traditional furniture looked several years old and worn, there was a flower patterned wallpaper in the dining room that she immediately wanted to tear down, and the thick curtains on the windows blocked out the sun. Despite the outdated decor, the layout of the downstairs was still charming, the hardwood floors and crown molding beautiful. Excitement bubbled inside of her as they entered the kitchen. With a few changes and staging, this house would be snatched up in a heartbeat.

The kitchen matched the rest of the house. Older

appliances and an apple theme. Apples adorned the curtains, the framed pictures on the wall and the tablecloth on the dinette table. Wesley pointed to a plate of cinnamon rolls on the tiled island. Bags of flour and sugar, along with a carton of eggs and containers of spices adorned the countertops.

Cierra looked from the island to Wesley. "You really did make the cinnamon rolls from scratch."

Wesley rubbed the back of his head and shrugged. "I did."

"I didn't know you could bake."

"I don't bake a lot. I stayed here last night and woke up with an urge to make cinnamon rolls. I used to help my mom make them when we were kids. When I'm here, I can't help myself." He avoided eye contact after he finished talking. Cierra hoped he wasn't embarrassed for revealing so much.

"That's really sweet. I'm a decent cook, but I can't bake a thing."

"I remember those brownies you brought to the bake sale," Wesley said in a dry voice.

Cierra groaned and pressed a hand to her forehead. "Don't remind me of those brownies. Rockhard lumps that the football team used for a throwing contest. It was my first huge failure in front of my peers."

Wesley shook his head. "I wouldn't say it was a failure. My friend Carlos won the throwing contest that day. So someone got a win."

His voice held the calm, I'm-not-invested-in-this-story tone he often used, but humor danced in his brown eyes. Her smile widened. She remembered this about Wesley. Always playing it cool as if he were above the drama, but still very much in tune to what was happening.

"Well, Carlos's win aside, I haven't baked anything that didn't have instructions on the box and only require heating for twelve to twenty minutes since then."

"That's good to hear. I'd hate to hear of you abusing more brownies like that," he said dryly.

Cierra laughed and playfully hit his shoulder. His full lips tilted up in that heart-stopping half grin again. Their eyes met, stuck, and Cierra's breathing stuttered. Heat spread through her neck and cheeks while delicious tingles danced across her skin.

Wesley looked away first and cleared his throat. "So, do we do this like at the DeWalt Manor? You just go around and take pictures?" His voice went back to the cool, disinterested tone from before.

Cierra didn't like the way he cooled so quickly. She liked the warmth that had crept into his eyes and voice before. Immediately, she wished she could slap some sense into herself. Hadn't she just said no fantasies about Wesley? That also meant no getting soft and gushy when he was nice to her.

She grabbed a cinnamon roll and took a bite. It was still warm and delicious. Cierra had to stop herself from drooling. She gave Wesley a thumbs-up. Pride brightened his eyes before he turned and got his own roll.

"Kind of like last time," she said after swallowing. "Already I can see some things you can do to make the house more marketable."

He turned to her with brows drawn together. "Things like what?"

"Well, the inside is outdated. I don't know how much you want to put into the home before selling. Even without making changes you'll sell quickly, but if you really want to get the highest offers, I'd suggest removing the old furniture. Maybe bringing in some newer furniture, rental of course, for staging before an open house. Otherwise, get rid of the older pieces to open up the place and let prospective buyers imagine the home as their own." She pointed toward the apple-themed curtains. "Take down all this apple stuff. Often appliances stay with the home, so I'd suggest updating at least the stove and fridge. Then there's the wallpaper in the dining room. I only caught a glimpse, but it should come down."

She took another bite of the cinnamon roll and met Wesley's eyes. He stood completely still and watched her with hard eyes. The bite she'd taken stuck in her throat. She was used to sellers feeling overwhelmed when she made recommendations, but the anger in his eyes... She wasn't expecting that.

She forced herself to swallow. "What's wrong?"

He dropped his roll on the plate and placed his hands on his hips. "What's wrong? You came all the way here to tell me what's wrong with my house?"

"I didn't come to tell you what's wrong. I came to give you suggestions to…update the place a bit." She tried to sound pleasant despite the obvious irritation on his face.

"That doesn't sound like 'updating the place a bit.'" He made air quotes with his fingers while saying the last part.

"It's not a criticism. I'm just doing my job."

"So your job is to come in and tell people all the terrible things about their homes?"

Cierra took a deep breath and pinched the bridge of her nose. She wanted to remain calm and professional, to not give Wesley the wrong idea about her, but he wasn't even listening to her explanation.

She dropped her hand and met his gaze. "It's all recommendations. You don't have to do any of that."

"But you don't think my house is good enough to sell as is?"

Cierra put her hands on her hips. Now he was being deliberately obtuse. "I'm giving my professional opinion of things that could make the house sell for more. But, again, if you didn't change a thing, we could still put the house on the market and get a good price."

"I'd hoped this would work out, but you're still the same."

Cierra's head tilted to the side. "What's that supposed to mean?"

He crossed his arms. "You're superficial and only focused on what looks good on the surface."

The anger she'd suppressed and tried to cover up with professional understanding boiled over until she didn't care how Wesley viewed her. Cierra took a step forward. "How dare you?"

"I dare because it's true. You were like that in high school, and I see that's the same now. You can't see the deeper meaning and are ready to get rid of perfectly good stuff just to go with something flashy."

Cierra threw the cinnamon roll. The pastry hit Wesley with a splat in the center of his chest before sliding down his shirt and plopping on the floor. "And you're still the judgmental asshole I remember you to be. I don't know what your problem is or why you decided to take my recommendations for your house and turn it into an assault on my character, but you picked the wrong one today. I don't need this or your help." She spun on her heel and marched out of the house.

Chapter Five

Wesley took a deep breath and clenched the clear plastic container in his hands as he stared at the door of Cierra's realty office. He'd expected her office to be located in a strip mall or other office complex, but when he'd pulled up her website and located the address, he was surprised to discover she worked out of a finished room over the garage of a single-family home. The office hours listed on her website ended at five. He'd hoped to catch her at the end of the day when she wasn't with a client.

Now, as he stared at the open sign on the door in front of him, he hesitated. He'd practiced all sorts of apologies for the way he'd acted the day before, but they all felt hollow. He'd been out of line, and she'd had every right to throw a cinnamon roll at him.

With a deep breath he opened the door to the office. A bell chimed and the smell of flowers greeted him. The interior had a living space that was used as the office and a small kitchenette area. He didn't see anyone inside. A white desk covered in papers sat in the back left corner of the office space. A whiteboard with multicolored notes about various listings hung on one wall. A small gray sofa and two blue accent chairs next to a small coffee table filled the other half of the space.

A small girl popped up from behind the desk and stared at him with wide eyes. Her hair was pulled into a puff at the top of her head and she was dressed in a Wonder Woman T-shirt. Wesley froze just inside the door. She watched him carefully but didn't speak.

Wesley glanced around the room for a sign of Cierra, but there was only the girl. "Um… Hello. I'm looking for Ms. Cierra Green."

The girl cocked her head to the side. "Are you a client?"

Wesley nodded slowly. "I am."

A smile brightened her cute face. "Are you going to sell a house so my mommy can make a lot of money?"

Wesley blinked. Mommy? Cierra had a daughter? He vaguely remembered hearing about Cierra and Troy having a kid, but he'd made a habit out of blocking out any information related to both of them. The fact that she lived outside of Sunshine Beach made not keeping up with her or Troy really easy.

"Maybe," he said. "If she still wants to sell my house."

The girl nodded. "She does. Mommy likes to

make money." She pointed to the sofa. "Please have a seat and she'll be right with you. She's in the...uh, I think she said to say indespised?"

Wesley moved to the sofa. "Indewhat?"

The door next to the kitchen area opened and Cierra walked out. She paused in the middle of wiping her hands on a paper towel as she caught a glimpse of him. Her brows rose and her full lips parted with surprise. She was dressed casually, in a sleeveless white button-up shirt and jeans. Her thick hair hung loose around her face but appeared disheveled. As if she'd run her hands through it several times. It made him think about how her hair would look if he ran his fingers through the silky strands after kissing her pouty lips.

"Wesley?" she asked, breaking him from the fantasy he had no business starting. "What are you doing here?"

Her daughter spoke up. "He's here to sell a house so you can make a lot of money. I told him you were indespised."

Cierra's lips lifted in a small smile. "That's *indisposed*, sweetie. Thank you."

The girl grinned. "You're welcome." The girl dropped back down behind the desk.

Wesley looked at the space Cierra's daughter disappeared from then back at Cierra. Cierra shrugged and chuckled.

"My daughter, Aria. She's coloring on the floor behind my desk."

He nodded. "Ah… I didn't know you had kids."

"I do." She crossed her arms and lifted her chin. "I was just about to lock up for the day." She didn't say it, but he heard the *what do you want* in her voice.

Clearing his throat, Wesley held out the container in his hands. "These are for you."

She eyed the container. "What's for me?"

"Cinnamon rolls." When her eyes widened, he lifted a shoulder. "My way of saying I'm sorry."

Her lips pursed in a cute way despite the *whatever* gleam in her dark eyes. "You're sorry for what?"

"For snapping at you the other day. The things you said, they were right."

"If you knew that, then why did you get mad?"

Wesley held himself still and met her stare even though he wanted to fidget beneath her scrutiny. Cierra could always unnerve him with just a look, smile or touch. "Everything you said needed to go are things that have been in the house since I was a kid. Things my parents put there. My brothers and I never changed anything. Your suggestions to get rid of it all hit a nerve. I didn't expect that, and I lashed out at you. I'm sorry."

The stiffness in her shoulders melted away. She threw the paper towel in her hand in a trash can by the door she'd exited and walked over to him. "Are you sure you want to sell? I know the house has a lot of meaning for you and your brothers. If you reacted like that, maybe you shouldn't sell."

Wesley shook his head. "Dion lives in Charlotte and now that we have the show Tyrone is jet-setting all over the country. I have my condo, which is all that I want. It's time to move on."

"Are you sure?"

Everyone else was moving on. Dion, who he'd never thought would leave, had moved away without a second glance. Tyrone had only stuck around because of Dion. Wesley was left with the responsibility of keeping things together. He was the only one holding on to the past. He wasn't going to be left behind.

"Yeah, I'm sure."

She watched him for several seconds then nodded. "Okay. Like I said, we don't have to do everything I recommended. Your house will sell quickly with no changes."

He'd considered what she'd said as he'd cleaned up the thrown cinnamon roll and later washed the icing off his shirt. Her suggestions hadn't been bad. Once he'd let go of the sentimental attachment and viewed things critically, he'd realized that. "I'd like to make small improvements. I'm not a home improvement person, that's Dion, but clearing some things out and staging I can handle. Will you help me?"

She cocked her head to the side. "Are you still helping me with the DeWalt Manor?"

"I am."

Her bright-as-the-sun smile came out. "Then, yes, I'll help you." She held up a finger before he could feel relief. "On one condition."

"What condition?"

She pointed to the container in his hand. "Are those homemade or did they come out of the refrigerated section?"

He pressed a hand to his chest. "Ma'am, I would not apologize with store-bought cinnamon rolls."

Cierra's laugh made him feel as if he were floating on air. "Great. Come over to the kitchen and let's heat one up."

Her daughter popped up from behind the desk again. "Can I get one?"

Cierra waved her over. "Of course you can."

Wesley followed Cierra and Aria to the kitchenette area. Aria's eyes widened and she licked her lips when Wesley opened the container to reveal the cinnamon rolls. Cierra leaned over the container and took a deep breath.

"Oh my God, Wesley, these smell better than the ones you made the other day." She pulled paper towels off the roll next to the sink.

"Thanks. The ones the other day were good, but they were also a last-minute decision. I took my time making these."

Her appreciative smile as she used a plastic fork to scoop out a roll onto paper towels made the extra care he'd put into the pastries worth every second.

"Can I warm mine up?" Aria asked.

"Put it in for ten seconds. That's all," Cierra answered.

Aria nodded and took her treat to the microwave. Wesley glanced around the office space.

"This is where you work, huh."

"It is." Cierra watched Aria as she punched in the time before looking back at Wesley. "When I bought the house, the room over the garage was a big selling point. I knew I wanted to start my own brokerage, but I can't afford office space, yet. It's a win-win."

"How long have you lived here?"

"About two years. After the divorce I lived with my parents until things got settled and I was able to buy the house."

He was curious to know what kind of things had to get settled. He was even more curious to know why she'd got divorced. Had the divorce left a sour taste in her mouth for relationships? Was she dating again?

Nah, bruh, you do not need to be worrying about that! The thought came immediately after the questions popped into his mind. He was not dating Cierra. They were working together. That's it.

Aria ran over and tapped his arm. "This is so

good!" Icing covered half of her face. "Can you bring some more?"

Cierra grabbed another paper towel and bent to wipe the icing from her daughter's face. "Aria, this was just Mr. Livingston being nice. He's a client and doesn't have to bring more rolls."

"I don't mind." The words came out before he had time to process his offer. Cierra's head snapped up as she looked at him surprised. Wesley cleared his throat and glanced away. "When I get in the mood to bake, it's always too much. I usually share with my brothers, but they aren't around. I'll add you to my homemade goods donation list." He looked back at her and gave a lazy shrug he hoped didn't make the promise to bring her baked goods sound like a big deal.

Cierra slowly straightened. The look in her eyes made him want to slide closer. There was a small bit of icing at the corner of her mouth. He lifted a hand but stopped short of touching her lips.

"You've got a bit of icing..." His voice trailed off when she poked out her tongue and licked her lips. Desire punched him in the gut. "Uh...you got it."

She lifted a hand quickly to her mouth and rubbed her lips. "Thanks. Also, thanks for the apology and adding me to your baked goods donation list."

"No problem at all." He kept his voice lighthearted. Wesley held Cierra's gaze. Something shot between them, something he knew damn well was attraction. Attraction he was afraid to even acknowledge. Deep down a warning went off. Working with Cierra was going to be a problem.

Chapter Six

Cierra sighed, gripped the steering wheel with one hand and rubbed her temple with the other. She was driving. She couldn't blow up. She had to remain calm.

"I'm sorry, Ms. Mack, but can you repeat that?" she asked, trying not to kill the messenger of this particular bad news.

"Sure." Ms. Mack's voice came through Cierra's car's Bluetooth soothing and slightly sympathetic. This wasn't the first time the director of Aria's after-school program had had to call. "Your balance is two weeks behind. I know you're typically good for it, but I can't make an exception."

"I understand. Do you still have my credit card information on file?" she asked.

"I do. Would you like me to use that card?"

"Please, and in the future if the account isn't paid for the week, please go ahead and run my card to avoid further delays."

"I'll be sure to make a note to the account."

"Thank you for your call. I'll do what I need to on my end to avoid this happening again."

Cierra pressed the button on her phone to disconnect the call. She wanted to hit something, so she punched the empty passenger seat. "Troy, you stupid son of a... Ugh!" she yelled out in the car before pressing the button and directing the voice command to call her manipulative, game-playing ex-husband.

As the phone rang, she tried to take calming breaths. She was driving. She couldn't behave irrationally. She couldn't drive to Troy's job, demand he come outside and run her car over him a dozen times.

"Cierra, hey, baby, what's up?" Troy's voice came through thick and gooey as artificial honey.

"Don't 'baby' me, Troy. Why didn't you pay Aria's after-school tuition? I just got a call from Ms. Mack, again. Do you want her kicked out?"

She cringed as soon as the words left her mouth. Of course he wanted Aria kicked out. He hadn't wanted her in after-school in the first place. He'd wanted Cierra at home, waiting for Aria with a healthy snack on the table, and the day's home-cooked meal warming in the oven in anticipation for him to arrive. That had been Troy's dream. The life she'd tried to comply with for twelve years that had slowly suffocated her.

"She wouldn't have to be in after-school care if you hadn't chosen to break up our family."

If she had a nickel for every time he came with that tired line… "Troy, let's not go there. Despite your feelings the divorce is final, and I've got the paperwork demanding you pay child support, which includes covering Aria's after-school care. If you miss it again, then I'm going to the court. It's been three years. I need you to stop acting like I'm coming back. I'm not and these games only remind me why I left in the first place."

"Come on, Cierra, don't be like that. I can't help it if you broke my heart."

"You know what you can help? You can help your daughter not get kicked out of the after-school program she loves. You can keep her from being embarrassed because she has to constantly get a late-payment slip put into her book bag. You can show her that you respect her mother even though we aren't married anymore. How about you focus on her needs instead of your hurt feelings? Our relationship is between us, and we've already hashed that out. Aria is the focus now. Can you remember that?"

"Why you trying to act like my feelings don't matter?" His fake, placating tone gave way to one of petulance.

"This call isn't about your feelings. This call is about paying for your daughter's after-school program on time. Can you do that from now on?"

He was silent for several seconds. "You know this is about more than that."

"No, it's not. It's been three years. Let's stop this."

"Come work for me. We can still be a team and if you're here, then you can remind me to pay for after-sc—"

"Goodbye, Troy." Cierra pressed the button to end the call. "Ugh!"

Troy liked having things his way. The happiness had already worn off their marriage but they'd kept trying to make things work for Aria's sake. Yet he'd acted surprised when Cierra walked away after learning about his financial indiscretions. If he would have pulled the plug on their marriage, he would have been fine, but because she'd called it quits first, his feelings were hurt.

Cierra was happy to be out of the relationship. She didn't regret her marriage—it had given her Aria, who was the most important thing in the world to her—but she did regret trying to make it last long after she realized she wasn't in love with Troy anymore, and she would never be able to fit the 1950s image he tried to place on her and their life together.

The divorce hadn't turned her off the idea of relationships. She wanted to date again. Longed to feel a man's arms around her, for her heart to skip with an excited beat of anticipation when someone came near, to spend late hours talking on the phone and all that other silly stuff people did at the start of a relationship. She wasn't ready to be married again, but she didn't believe that just because her marriage failed that she was forever out of luck in the relationship department.

An image of Wesley drifted into her head. His small smile as he'd offered the cinnamon rolls with his apology. How nice his forearms looked when he'd held up the container. The way he'd been sweet and patient with Aria as she asked him if he was going to sell a house so her mommy could make more money. He was the kind of guy she could see herself starting over with.

Cierra gasped and slapped her forehead several times. "Nope. Stop. Don't go there. Not with Wesley Livingston."

"I don't really like her. I just said I'd go because she asked. She's not my type."

Sure, the words were spoken over a decade ago, but the humiliation and pain that had burst through her after overhearing Wesley admit that to a group of his friends after she'd asked him to the prom had been very real and cut very deep. Not only had she heard, but so had two of her friends from the cheerleading squad. They'd promised not to tell anyone, and thankfully they'd never revealed her humiliation to the rest of the team or the school, but Cierra hadn't been able to look at Wesley again without remembering the disdain in his voice. He may have grown and changed, but she'd tap-danced and played nice to make one man happy for years. She wasn't about to try to figure out what Wesley liked and mold herself into that image. She deserved more than that.

Fifteen minutes after her call with Troy, Cierra arrived at Wesley's family home. She'd shaken off most of the irritation from her conversation with Troy and forced a bright, I-can-sell-this-house smile onto her face when she rang the bell. She let out a surprised chuckle when he answered wearing a faded blue apron with apples printed on it over a pair of gray joggers and a dark blue T-shirt. He held a duster in one hand and a red checkered rag in the other. But it was the clear plastic cap on his head that made him absolutely adorable.

She brought a hand to her lips in an attempt to suppress her laughter. "Did you forget I was coming?"

Wesley shook his head. "Nah, I remembered. I was dusting. I thought I'd at least clean things up and let you see the house in its full glory before you came in and made suggestions." He stepped back and Cierra entered.

She pointed to his head. "Do you always wear a plastic cap when you dust?"

"Huh?" He brought a hand to his head. His eyes

widened. "Oh!" He snatched the cap off. "I forgot I had that on. I dusted the ceiling fans."

"And you couldn't get dust in your hair?" she teased.

His lips lifted in a heart-stopping grin. "I just got my hair cut this morning," he said by way of an explanation.

Cierra held up a hand. "Hey, I get it. You gotta protect a fresh cut."

"You know it. Come on in."

He led her into the living room, where the scent of lemon furniture polish greeted them. Everything gleamed in the sunlight filtering through the windows. Windows draped by curtains she still thought needed to be replaced. She glanced around the room and admitted there was a charm to the formal living space. The big traditional furniture and thick wood coffee table and side table were outdated but still looked comfortable.

She gasped and pointed. "Is that a touch lamp?" She walked over and touched the gold base. Light illuminated behind the frosted glass shade with blue painted flowers. She tapped the lamp twice more to bring the light to its brightest.

Wesley laughed. "Yeah, I think it belonged to my grandma or an auntie or something. I remember when my mom brought it home and said it would be perfect for the living room. Me and my brothers would touch it so much Mom finally banned us from the living room."

Cierra smiled at the memory and turned back to him. "I don't blame her. I can only imagine the threat you and your brothers were to her newest prize." She looked around the room and then back at him. "This is a nice space. I think if we clear out a few things it'll work, but the lamp has to stay."

Wesley put the duster and rag on the coffee table and crossed his arms. "I know that a lot of the things in here are out of style now. Now that I've come to terms with everything, I'll be okay. Tell me what you think, and we'll make it work. I've even rented a storage space for everything we need to clear out."

She rubbed the back of her neck. "Are you sure?" She didn't want a repeat of the last time she'd come here.

"I'm sure."

"What about your brothers?"

Wesley's gaze skipped away for a beat before returning to hers. "They left me in charge of the house."

"Do they know you're *selling* the house?"

"They know I'm taking care of things." He pointed over his shoulder. "Let's check out the rest of the place."

He tried to walk by her out of the living room. Cierra grabbed on to the strings of the apron and pulled. Wesley stumbled backward. Her arms shot up to try and catch him so he wouldn't fall, but he was nimble on his feet. He swiveled to face her and balanced himself in one fluid movement. Her hands landed in the middle of his chest. She wasn't sure if it was the momentum or her being so close, but he braced himself with his hands on her hips.

They froze in that position. Their gazes locked. His dark brown eyes dropped to her mouth. His heartbeat increased beneath her palms on his chest. He smelled a little like the lemon furniture polish and the spicy blend of a body wash or cologne. Instead of clashing, the scents mingled into an enticing blend. Cierra sucked in short shallow breaths as she watched him. His eyes slowly rose back to hers. For a second, she hoped he'd pull her closer and press her against this body.

Wesley hastily let her go and stepped back. "My bad."

Cierra let out a shaky breath. Her cheeks were hot and her breasts felt heavy. She rubbed her neck and looked at the faded apples on his apron versus meeting his gaze. "No, my bad. I was the one who pulled on you."

"Why?"

"Huh?"

"Why did you pull on the strings?"

She unscrambled the thoughts in her brain and tried to remember. "Your brothers. They don't know you're selling, do they?"

He waved a hand. "It'll be fine."

"You keep saying that, but shouldn't you talk to them first? Not just because when I list this place everyone in town will know, but because they need to know what you're doing."

He shook his head and his eyes hardened. "They'll be fine. I know what I'm doing. This is for the best."

"I'm serious, Wesley. I don't want to get in the middle of something. I'd feel better if your brothers knew about—"

He stepped closer to her and placed his hands on her forearms. Cierra's eyes widened and she sucked in a breath. He stared into her eyes and gave her a quick nod. "I've got it. I wouldn't call you in and mess with your money like that. Don't worry. You help me spruce this place up and show my brothers what we can get, and they'll be on board." He did the cocky chin raise coupled with an I-got-this eye gleam that he'd used back when they were chemistry lab partners and she'd worry about how their experiment would turn out. Just like then, it made her heart flip. "I got you. Aight?"

Not all right. The guy had scattered all her thoughts and made her want to swoon with just a look and a smile. She should insist that he call his brothers now. She should walk away until she could meet with all three.

"Oh, by the way, I got more information on the DeWalt Manor," he said. "Let's talk about it after we go through the house." He squeezed her hip then stepped back.

The manor, her reason for agreeing to sell it, along with the benefit she'd get for selling his place came back. He did need to know his options when he talked to his brothers. Besides, she was here to make money, not figure out what was going on with Wesley and his brothers. She nodded. "Sounds good!"

Chapter Seven

Wesley looked from the pile of boxes on the back of the moving truck to his brother Dion standing next to him. Dion was the tallest of the three, with a smooth bald head currently covered by a Charlotte Hornets ball cap. Like Wesley and Tyrone, Dion was dressed in a pair of old jeans and a T-shirt that wouldn't be mourned if they were ruined while they worked.

Wesley rubbed his jaw. "Remind me again why you didn't hire movers?"

Tyrone laughed and slapped Wesley on the shoulder. He was half an inch shorter than Wesley and wore a black sweatband around the edges of his stylish fade to keep the sweat out of his dark eyes. "Because our big brother hates to pay someone to do something he thinks he can do himself."

Wesley pointed at Dion. "I'm gonna need you to realize that hiring help is not a weakness."

Dion waved off Wesley's words before stepping into the back of the moving truck. "Come on, fellas, this won't take us long at all."

Wesley suppressed a sigh before reaching up and taking the box Dion handed down. When Dion texted asking for help moving into the new house he and his girlfriend, Vanessa, were renting, Wesley had quickly said yes since he hadn't seen his brothers since filming ended. In his enthusiasm for male bonding, he'd forgotten how much he hated moving. A mistake he'd regret when his back ached later.

Tyrone took the next box Dion handed down. "I want a hundred wings after this."

Wesley shifted his box. "Make that two hundred. I'm already starving."

Dion only grinned as he slid a large box toward the edge of the truck before hopping down. "You know good and damn well you can't eat that much." He reached back and slid the box into his arms.

Tyrone lifted a brow. "Nah, man, I'm trying to eat for the rest of the week. You owe us that much."

Wesley nodded and readjusted the heavy box in his arms. "I agree."

"Greedy suckas," Dion said with mock disgust. "Fine, I'll order you all the damn wings you want. Now help me unload this truck."

Two and a half hours later the truck was unloaded, and the boxes and small amount of furniture Dion and Vanessa previously had in her apartment were safely deposited in the two-bedroom home. Dion complied with his brothers' demands and ordered enough wings to feed a football team along with fries and soda. The three spread a sheet on the living room floor, since the new dining room table Vanessa ordered wasn't being delivered for another week and gathered around the food to enjoy.

"When does Vanessa get off?" Wesley asked right after piling his plate with an assortment of wings.

Dion glanced at his cell phone. "She'll probably get home around five or six. She had to fill in for the weekend anchor and it may take her a little longer to get out."

Tyrone nodded. "At least we got everything done before she got home."

"True," Dion said. "She's going to be pleasantly surprised to find everything out of the truck."

Wesley glanced around the house then back at Dion. "You want any of the furniture out of the family house?"

Dion shook his head. "Nah, Vanessa wants new furniture for our new start and I'm actually good with that. No need to keep the old furniture from the house."

Wesley laughed softly and shook his head.

Dion's brows drew together. "Why you laughing?"

"It's nothing much, just something Cierra said." When his brothers both gave him a quizzical look, Wesley continued. "She said the furniture in the house was old-fashioned. That's all."

Tyrone's eyes narrowed. "What she doing in the house?"

Wesley froze for a second. He had planned to tell his brothers about his plans to sell the family home, but he hadn't meant to blurt things out. He wanted to get an idea of how much of a fuss they'd make and work on updating the place before springing it on them. That way they'd have no room for argument and would see the benefits of his decision.

"You know I'm helping her investigate the De-Walt Manor. She came by one day and we talked about it." He'd texted his brothers after the first visit to the manor. They'd been so enthusiastic about investigating the home that they'd immediately called back to learn more. For now, since it wasn't for the show and he didn't want to scare off Carolyn De-Walt, Wesley asked his brothers to let him handle the investigation. He'd call them in if he needed them later.

Tyrone's eyes lit up with interest. "How's that going? Man, I wish we could've got their permission to investigate the house for the show."

Wesley relaxed as the curiosity about another ghost investigation took his brother's mind off Cierra visiting. "I went with her to talk to the owner about the listing. There is something going on in that house. I could feel it, but what's weird is I didn't feel what the owner says guests reported encountering."

Dion took a swig of his soda then asked, "What did they feel?"

"Anger, animosity, rage. Whoever is there scares them. But when I was there, I didn't get any of that. I mean, I sensed some anger, but mostly what I felt was… I don't know. Almost anticipation. I think whoever is there has something to say."

Tyrone twisted his lips and pointed at Wesley with one of his honey mustard wings. "Something to say and it's probably about that family. What's the history?"

"I haven't got to dig in much," Tyrone answered. "They say that even though the home was once a plantation that nothing traumatic ever happened there."

Tyrone sucked his teeth. "If there was nothing traumatic, they wouldn't have an angry spirit."

Dion tilted his head toward Tyrone and smirked. "Facts." He looked at Wesley. "You sure you don't want us to come down when you use the EMF and try to communicate?"

Wesley shook his head. "Y'all don't have to do that."

Tyrone pressed a hand to his chest. "Why not? That's what we do."

"I'm just saying, y'all have been busy." Wesley pointed at Dion. "You've got the new job." He jerked his chin in Tyrone's direction. "And you're busy jet-setting around the country promoting the show."

Tyrone held up a finger. "I'm just doing some preliminary stuff to get our names out there. You know that before the premiere we're all going to have to do the promos for the show."

Wesley wiped his hands with a napkin and nodded. "I know."

Tyrone reached over and slapped his arm. "Don't sound so worried. This was our dream. We're here. We got a show and everything. This is a blessing."

Dion nodded. "It is."

"I know that," Wesley agreed. "I'm excited, but you know I'm not good with all the extra attention."

Dion shrugged in a no-big-deal kind of way. "Just remember that we know what we do and why. Talking about the show is no different than talking to any of the people we help."

"Still, it's not the same when it's going to be on television. Sometimes I miss the way things were before we got the show. Y'all were still around, and we could just get up and go on the weekend to do an investigation."

Dion met Wes's eyes. "We can still do that. We're still around. That's why we offered to help with the DeWalt Manor."

"I know you say that, but I don't want Carolyn DeWalt to think we're trying to use this for the show. Besides, you don't have time." He glanced at Tyrone. "And are you coming back to stay in Sunshine Beach?"

Tyrone shrugged. "I don't know. I'm thinking of letting my lease expire."

"See what I mean," Wesley said, some of the frustration of being left behind entering his voice.

"Whether we move away or not doesn't change anything," Dion said in his father-figure, I've-got-us voice. The one he'd adopted the second he'd decided to give up a scholarship to play college football and stay home to keep all of them together after their parents died. "We're doing the show together and we'll still investigate together. If any of you need anything, you know I'm there, right?"

"Of course," Tyrone said instantly. "The same for me."

Wesley took a long breath and nodded. "I know. It's why I'm up here helping you move boxes and furniture."

His brothers laughed before they got quiet and ate more food. After a few seconds Wesley asked hesitantly, "You ever thought about selling the family house? I mean…since we all are doing different things."

Tyrone and Dion both stilled. Wesley held his breath and waited. They'd pretty much confirmed they weren't going to stay in Sunshine Beach. The house wasn't what had kept them together. Maybe he'd worried about how they'd react for no reason.

Dion spoke first. "Yeah, I mean, I've thought about it."

Tyrone nodded. "Same. It's a lot to maintain."

Wesley's hopes rose. He opened his mouth to tell them about what Cierra said but Dion chimed in.

"But let's worry about what to do with the house another day. For now, let's focus on the series premiere and go from there."

Tyrone waved a finger. "Exactly what I was gonna say."

Wesley wanted to keep the conversation going but decided not to push. They were at least open to selling and the two had both considered it. Even though they hadn't outright agreed, Wesley felt more confident in his decision. He'd keep working with Cierra, get the house ready and give his brothers an offer they couldn't refuse.

Chapter Eight

Cierra waved at Wesley from the front of Carolina Home Furnishings. The locally owned furniture store was located away from Sunshine Beach in the revitalized riverfront area, a popular shopping area for locals and tourists. She'd watched while he parked his car in one of the spaces along the busy street and looked toward the store. He caught sight of her waving. He grinned and waved back.

Something about that simple gesture made her stomach flip. Maybe it was because he looked happy to see her. He probably was simply happy she'd agreed to help him get an idea of what kind of furniture he could use to stage his home. Whereas she was just happy to see him.

He'd dressed casually in a black T-shirt and gray pants, both of which fit his tall frame perfectly. As he drew closer and his smile broadened, the breath stuck in her throat. He walked right up to her, and she instinctively leaned in and opened her arms to hug him. What could she say? She was a hugger. She was from a family of huggers and Wesley nearing her with that heart-stopping smile and the warm look in his eye made her react physically if not smartly. Just as she was about to drop her arms and go for the awkward handshake instead, he surprised her by leaning closer and wrapping one arm around her shoulder.

"What's up, Cierra?" he said in an easy voice.

Cierra breathed in the delicious smell of his cologne. The hardness of his chest pressed into her breasts and warmth spread from her stomach up into her chest and neck and downward into the sensitive spot between her thighs.

She quickly pulled back and brushed the hair behind her ears. "Hey, you made it."

His smile didn't go away. "I asked you to meet me."

She looked toward the sky and lightly hit the side of her head. "Duh, I know that." She laughed clumsily. Good grief, she was making a fool out of herself. Over one damn hug that she'd initiated. "How's your day going?"

"Pretty good. You?"

She gave two thumbs-up. "I'm great. Ready to go inside and check out some furniture?"

"That's why I asked you here."

"Right." She let out another laugh that sounded way too loud. "Let's go." She spun quickly and turned to the door. As soon as her back was to him she cringed. What the hell was wrong with her?

She'd already had the no-getting-romantic-ideas-about-Wesley talk with herself. The man was not interested in her like that. He hadn't been when they were younger, and he wasn't showing any interest now. Once again, she was getting herself all excited about something that wasn't going to happen.

Wesley reached around her and opened the door. The movement brought him closer so she was once again teased by his cologne and the warmth of his body. She nodded her thanks and hurried inside the store.

One of the salespeople, a curvy white woman with short dark hair wearing a gray suit, smiled at them and came over. "Welcome to Carolina Home Furnishings. Is there anything I can help you with?"

Cierra shook her head. "We're just looking for now. Trying to get some ideas for a living and dining room."

The saleswoman pointed toward the back of the store. "No problem. Most of our living and dining items are in that area. If you have any questions, just let me know. My name is Sarah."

"Thanks, Sarah," Wesley said. He put his hand on the small of Cierra's back and led her in the direction Sarah indicated.

Cierra picked up the pace until Wesley's hand fell away. She liked the slight pressure and warmth of his hand on her back a bit too much. Liked it so much she wanted him to run his hand up her back, wrap it around her shoulder and pull her into his side. But if he did that, then they would be like a real couple out shopping for furniture together and this wasn't about being a real couple.

She caught sight of a nice sectional and pointed. "What do you think of this? It would look good in the living room."

Wesley walked over and studied the beige-colored furniture. "It's nice. I like the entire setup. The coffee table and lamps, too."

"You cannot give up the touch lamps," she said, placing her hand on his arm. "Those things are classic."

He laughed and shook his head. "No way could I give up the lamps."

"Sectionals are popular right now, but a more traditional setup would work, too. I'll show you some other ideas."

They walked through the store and Cierra pointed out which styles of sofas would open the space in his living room but also give it a warm, welcoming feel that new buyers would enjoy. Wesley took in her suggestions without a hint of animosity or concern, unlike when she'd first mentioned removing the older furniture.

When he sat on a sofa with power reclining seats, she said, "I'm glad you're open to the ideas. I wasn't sure if you were really okay with removing some of the old furniture."

He bounced on the sofa's leather seats to test it out as he'd done with every other chair he'd sat in. "What you said was right. I even brought it up to my brothers and they admitted they'd considered getting rid of some things." He leaned over and searched the side of the chair.

"Did you talk to them about selling the house?"

He ran his hand over the outside of the chair and frowned. "They're good."

"Really? I wondered if they'd be resistant."

She could barely keep the relief out of her voice. She'd tamped down her expectations of selling Wesley's house after getting the feeling his brothers weren't on board. But after a week of trying to recruit new agents, only to have them say no or go with a more big-name organization, like her ex-husband's, she really wanted to be the one to list Wesley's home. That and the DeWalt Manor would go a long way to building trust in her abilities.

"Don't worry about my brothers. I've got them." Wesley didn't look at her as he leaned farther over the side of the chair as if he were looking for something.

Cierra frowned and stepped forward. "What are you doing?"

"Looking for the switch to activate the recline."

"Oh. It's right here." She bent forward to touch the button on the inner arm of the sofa.

Wesley sat up at the same time and bumped into

her side. Cierra lost her balance and wobbled on her feet. Wesley quickly reached up and took ahold of her arm to steady her. She looked up to thank him for stopping her fall but froze. Only the barest of inches separated them. She was close enough to see the dark circles of his pupils, which dilated as their eyes met. Electricity crackled across her skin for several tense seconds before his eyes lowered to her lips.

The need to lean forward and brush her lips across his rammed into her with the force of a wrecking ball. So hard and fast she sucked in a breath. Stunned and embarrassed for wanting to straddle Wesley in the middle of a furniture store, Cierra pressed the button for the recliner. She only meant to tap it to snap them both out of whatever trance they were being sucked into, but she hit the button too hard, and the bottom of the chair jerked out. It hit her leg and she toppled forward into Wesley's lap.

His breath rushed out as she landed on him. He caught her and laughed.

Heat flamed in Cierra's cheeks. She slapped his chest. "Don't laugh."

He stopped, but his body still vibrated with his suppressed humor. "I can't help it. What were you doing?"

She pointed to the button on the inside arm of the sofa. "I was trying to show you how to activate the recline. What else would I be doing?"

Wesley shifted so she wasn't in a weird angle and her butt nestled perfectly against the bulge between his legs. His humor immediately faded and awareness hummed between them. He'd rested one hand on the top of her thigh and his fingers tightened slightly. Cierra's arm around his shoulder tensed. Her gaze followed the slow bob of his Adam's apple as he swallowed hard. Cierra's sex clenched as desire swirled through her midsection.

"Cierra and Wesley, I thought that was you two." A woman's voice interrupted the moment.

Both Cierra and Wesley jumped and turned. A short older woman, with tawny brown skin wearing a red Montgomery Family Reunion T-shirt and jean capri pants watched them.

"Oh, Mrs. Montgomery, hi!" Cierra jumped off Wesley's lap as if it had suddenly caught fire. "I'm just helping Wesley find a sofa."

Arletha Montgomery's lips twitched, and her dark eyes sparked with humor. She crossed her arms and raised a brow. "I see you two finally met up."

Mrs. Montgomery was the one who'd given Cierra's mom the information about where Cierra could find Wesley. "Um, yeah, we did."

Wesley stood and came forward. He leaned down and gave the older woman a hug. "How are you doing, Mrs. Montgomery?"

She hugged him back tightly and patted his back. "I'm doing good. Are you helping Cierra with that

DeWalt place? I was hoping you would help them out the way you helped me."

Wesley straightened and nodded. "I am."

Cierra glanced between the two of them. "He helped you?"

Mrs. Montgomery beamed proudly at Wesley. "He did. Him and his brothers helped me get closure and I'll always be grateful for that. As soon as your mom told me about your problem selling the DeWalt Manor and that you were trying to contact Wesley I had to tell her where he likes to hide. Even though I don't care much for the DeWalt family, I'll always look out for Olivia and her girls."

"Do you know a lot about the DeWalt family?" Wesley asked.

Arletha shook her head. "An old friend of mine used to work for Carolyn's grandmother, but she passed away a few years ago. She said the family had secrets even though she wouldn't get into it."

Cierra leaned closer. "Secrets?"

Arletha sighed and shrugged. "Would you expect they didn't? I hope you figure out what's happening there, if only to give peace to whatever poor soul is sticking around."

Cierra smiled. "With Wesley's help I'm sure I will."

"I'll do my best," Wesley agreed.

Mrs. Montgomery's eyes narrowed. "But if you're helping her with the DeWalt Manor, why is she helping you find a couch?"

Wesley pointed toward the couch. "I'm thinking of updating my parents' place. Cierra mentioned she's got a little know-how on interior design from her work as a Realtor, so she agreed to help me out."

A knowing smile creased Arletha's face. "Is that the only reason?"

Cierra held up three fingers of her right hand. "Scout's honor. That's the only reason. We're just working together. That's all."

Arletha lifted a brow and continued to smirk. "If you say so. By the way, did your mom tell you about the fundraiser for the Literacy Council?"

Cierra's mom served on the board of directors for the Sunshine Beach Literacy Council. A group that Arletha was also a part of. "You mean the table at the farmer's market?"

Her mom had asked Cierra and Cetris about the council sponsoring a table at the local farmer's market to drum up membership and interest in their various events. She'd also asked them to help out at the table a few weekends. According to her mom, it would be another good way for Cierra to "get her face out there" in the community and build her business.

"Not just that. We're holding an adult prom to raise money for the library expansion," Arletha said with an excited wave of her hand.

"Oh yeah. The prom." Cierra's memory clicked. Her mom had mentioned that a while back. When she'd suggested Cierra bring Troy, she'd decided not to attend.

"Exactly. Valeria Murphy's daughter mentioned buying a fancy dress the other week even though she doesn't have anywhere to wear it. That gave us the idea to hold the prom fundraiser. It'll give everyone in town a chance to finally wear all those nice dresses and suits they've got sitting in the closet. Don't you think that's cute?"

Cierra could see the appeal. Lord knew she had a few nice dresses she'd purchased just because and had nowhere to go in them. In the years since her divorce, she hadn't got dressed up in anything fancier than a business suit to impress clients or potential agents to work for her.

"It's a good idea."

Arletha pointed at Cierra and Wesley. "Maybe you two can come to the prom together. I think you'd be cute together."

The comment landed like a grenade at Cierra's feet, blowing away the lightheartedness of the encounter with the reminder of the disaster that was her first attempt to go to prom with Wesley.

Arletha's phone rang and she pulled it out of her purse. "Oh, that's Valeria now. I'll see you two later. Don't forget to purchase your prom tickets." She waved and rushed toward the front of the store.

Cierra watched Mrs. Montgomery walk away and rubbed the back of her neck. She glanced at the couch where a few minutes ago she'd tumbled into Wesley's lap and nearly swooned. She bit her lip and suppressed a groan. She had to stop being a fool for Wesley Livingston.

"Um…you want to look at anything else?"

"No," Wesley said quickly. "I'm done. You ready?" His voice had lost the warmth and friendliness it held just moments before.

Cierra both wished Mrs. Montgomery hadn't mentioned any type of prom and was thankful she had. Wesley had only pretended to like her when she asked him to prom in high school. The comment brought back the embarrassment of knowing she'd been head over heels in love with Wesley back then and he'd only viewed her as a friend. A girl who wasn't his type. Just because he was nice to her now and they could laugh and joke didn't mean anything had changed.

They were silent as they walked out of the store. Wesley stopped once they were outside and faced her. His eyes didn't quite meet hers.

"Thanks again for meeting me here. I've got some good ideas," he said.

"Sure thing. If there's anything else you need for the house, let me know."

He shook his head. "You don't have to do anything extra to help me."

She smiled despite the stiffness in his voice. "It's nothing extra. I try to help all my clients. And, seeing as how I only have two clients right now, I've got plenty of time."

Wesley's brows drew together, and his eyes met hers. "You only have two clients?"

"For now. I sold a few houses before this, and I've got some recommendations from those people. Once I get your house on the market and sell the DeWalt Manor, then I'm hoping I can entice a few other agents to join my company. That will help."

He stared at her with a slight frown on his face. She shouldn't have blurted out how much she was struggling to keep her brokerage afloat. She was trying to instill confidence in her abilities, not make him doubt her.

"But I've got you covered. Don't worry." She gave him a bright smile and a thumbs-up. He may not see her as datable, but she'd be damned if she let him view her as incompetent.

He glanced away quickly, cleared his throat and shifted his stance. "I believe you. If anything, you were always good at getting what you wanted."

Cierra blinked. Was that a compliment or did he mean something else? When he'd got mad at her before at his place, he'd accused her of always going for the shiny thing. She'd been so angry at the time she hadn't thought to push him on that.

He looked back at her. "My brothers offered to help with the investigation if I need it."

She perked up. "Oh good. Do you think you'll need them?"

"I'm not sure. I'll start on my own and see what I figure out before dragging them away from their new lives." The way he'd said the last part… Was that resentment in his voice?

"I'm going back out there tomorrow," she said. "Some of the pictures I took didn't come out right and I need to retake them."

"What was wrong?"

"They came out super blurry or with weird lighting. I thought everything was good when I took them, but I guess not."

He shifted forward and his gaze lightened with interest. "Can I see them?"

"Sure." She pulled out her cell phone and navigated to the pictures. She ignored the way her heart rate picked up as Wesley stood closer to look at the images. "See what I mean?"

He reached out and held on to her phone. His hand engulfed hers as he pulled the cell up to get a better look. He pointed at the screen. "Cierra, that's not bad lighting. That's a spirit."

Her racing heart from his hand on hers was forgotten as his words sunk in. "For real?" Cierra squinted at the screen.

"For real." His eyes lit up and excitement filled his voice. "I knew I felt something in that room and you actually caught it on camera. What time are you going tomorrow? I'll come with you."

"I was going early in the day. I already spoke to Carolyn and she said she wouldn't be there but I should use the key to get in."

He frowned for a minute as if thinking, then gave a firm nod. "I can move some stuff around. Let me know when you're heading that way and I'll meet you there."

She nodded and grinned. She was not going to think about how excited she was to see him again tomorrow. "Sure."

"Will you text me those pictures?"

"I will."

He smiled at her. One of his full-on, you've-made-my-day smiles that made her want to jump into his arms and kiss those luscious lips. Instead, she backed away and gave him a thumbs-up. "I just remembered that I've got to be somewhere. I'll text and see you tomorrow." She turned and hurried to her car before Wesley saw the remnants of her schoolgirl crush in her eyes.

Chapter Nine

"What do you think we'll hear?"

Wesley looked up from the spirit box in his hand, a device that used radio frequencies to communicate with ghosts, at Cierra standing next to him. They were in the downstairs sitting room of the De-Walt Manor and he'd gone over the various equipment he used while investigating. Cierra asked a ton of questions, which he answered patiently. Her enthusiasm and interest in the investigation nearly matched his own.

Her interest almost made him forget he was mad at himself for letting his guard down and flirting with her the day before. Mad that he'd let that flirting lead him to almost kissing her. In the middle of a damn furniture store.

High school was a long time ago. He'd assumed any feelings from that time would fade and change, just like his perfect seventeen-year-old abs. Wasn't that what happened in the real world? Instead, the attraction lingered, wrapped around him and squeezed tight. Not just the attraction. He'd liked

Cierra back then. Liked her smile, the way she'd teased him, the way she'd seen him as Wesley and not just the middle brother. He liked her now as an adult. Her optimism, confidence and strength. As an adult he was beginning to weigh his teenage hurt feelings against his body's reaction to her now.

Cierra scooted even closer to take a better look at the spirit box. Her breasts pressed against his arm. He was already having a hard time not being distracted by her curves. Since they were investigating, she'd dressed casually in a loose tank top and shorts that stopped midthigh, yet Wesley could barely keep his eyes off all her smooth brown skin and imagined the softness hinted at beneath her clothes. The fragrance of whatever body wash she wore mixed with her own unique scent and lingered and caressed his senses like a lover's touch.

"I've never talked to a spirit before," Cierra said. "I didn't know you could do that."

Wesley shifted to his left and put a few centimeters' distance between him and Cierra. "Um... maybe a word or two. It's not a long conversation. I typically ask yes-or-no questions or things that can be answered easily."

"Oh, okay. Either way it's still pretty cool. I'm surprised Carolyn didn't want to sit in on this."

"I'm actually kind of glad she declined," Wesley said.

"Why?" Cierra cocked her head to the side and

looked up at him with those beautiful bright eyes of hers.

"The last time I was here the energy felt different whenever she was around. Whoever is lingering, I don't think they like her very much."

She cringed and bit the corner of her full lower lip. "If that's the case, why aren't they trying to get her out of here and make it easier to sell the place?"

Wesley shrugged. "Maybe we'll be able to find out."

"Do you feel any type of energy now?" She lowered her voice and held a hand up to her mouth as if she were relaying some secret.

He grinned despite himself. She was so cute, but it wasn't as if whispering would keep whoever was in the house with them from hearing. "I felt it the moment we came in."

Cierra became statue still. Her eyes darted around the room. "Like, right now?"

"Yeah."

She grabbed his arm and pressed against him. "Why didn't you tell me?"

Wesley chuckled. "You can't be scared. You were just excited a moment ago."

"That's because I didn't think anything was in here with us." Her fingers dug into his upper arm. "Where is it?"

He considered shaking her off. Having her this close was making concentration next to impossible.

Yet, the cautious look in her eye made him want to calm her.

"I can't see spirits," he said in a reassuring voice. "I just feel a presence. Here, you take my phone and record while I ask a few questions. Carolyn hasn't given us permission to use footage for the show, but I can still send what we find to my brothers and see what they think. They'll be interested, too."

She nodded and took his cell phone from him. The wariness in her eyes faded a little while he showed her where to stand and helped her put his camera in the tripod he'd brought to keep the camera steady. As he'd hoped, the distraction eased her discomfort.

He stood in front of the camera and looked back to Cierra. She gave him a thumbs-up. "I'm ready."

He nodded and turned on the spirit box. The sound of static filled the room. Wesley licked his lips and shifted from foot to foot. He wished Tyrone and Dion were here for this, but they'd have to be happy with seeing the video later.

"I'm Wesley and this is Cierra," he said. He glanced around the room as he spoke. "We're just here to talk. Is there someone here with us?"

He waited and listened. After a few seconds of nothing, he spoke again. "Can you tell us your name?"

The sound of the static from the spirit box filled the room. For the briefest second the sound changed.

Cierra gasped. Wesley's head jerked up and he stared at her. She had a hand over her mouth.

"Did you hear that?" she said. "I thought I heard *Mary*."

Wesley nodded. "I did, too."

She bit her lower lip, her eyes wide as she wrapped her arms around herself. Wesley pointed to the camera. "The camera still good?"

She dropped her arms and focused on the screen again. She gave him a thumbs-up. "Yeah. All good."

Satisfied that she was okay, he went back to asking questions. After several minutes of trying to communicate, Wesley was fairly sure that whomever Mary was, she wasn't alone, and they weren't happy with the home being sold. When the energy in the room disappeared, he and Cierra went to other parts of the house. They continued through the house where he got similar results. In every room he still felt welcome and nothing like the angry energy Carolyn described before.

They entered the kitchen last, and Wesley stopped in his tracks. Cierra, walking behind him, bumped into his back. He turned around and placed a hand on her arm to steady her.

"What's wrong?" she asked.

He shook his head and glanced around the kitchen. The hairs on the back of his neck stood up, and goose bumps tightened the skin on his arms. "Something's not right."

Cierra stiffened next to him. "Something like what?"

She shifted closer to him and grabbed on to the side of his shirt. The pain, animosity and heartache filling the air and pressing against him was stifling. His body tensed and his heart rate picked up. The emotions put him on the defensive. His fingers tightened around the box and he glanced around, knowing the room was empty yet feeling threatened.

"I don't exactly know." He turned on the spirit box. Instead of asking Cierra to set up the tripod like before, he let her continue to hold on to his shirt as he eased farther into the kitchen. He preferred having her close as his discomfort and unease rose. This was much more than the hint of anger he'd felt the last time they were there. It hadn't been this strong, but it had been there. The deep hurt beneath the curiosity. This had to be the same feeling affecting Carolyn and her family.

"I think we're finally going to meet the one behind the bad vibes in this place," he said softly.

Cierra's fingers clenched on his shirt, and she eased so close she nearly pressed into his side. "All right, that doesn't sound like fun."

"Let's see if we can find out why." Wesley licked his lips and took a deep breath before speaking into the room. "Can you tell us why you're angry?"

Both he and Cierra stood frozen, barely breathing as they waited for a reply. Sweat beaded on his fore-

head and slid down his cheek. After several agoniz-
ing seconds, Wesley's heart jumped into his throat
and Cierra shivered when something that sounded
a lot like *murder* echoed in the room.

Wesley rang Cierra's doorbell at seven that eve-
ning. He hadn't been able to shake his unease after
witnessing the look on her face when they'd left the
DeWalt Manor earlier that day. She'd obviously been
upset by the encounter. Her usually bright personality was dimmed, her smile forced and the vibrant
tone of her voice diminished.

He'd tried to distract himself by calling his brothers and telling them what he'd found. They'd been
excited and eager to get back into town to investigate with him, but since they hadn't received the
official okay from Carolyn, Wesley decided to
continue to be the only one visible at the property.
After talking to his brothers, he'd tried to get lost
in the new horror novel he'd downloaded but with
every tense moment in the book he kept thinking of
Cierra, the way she'd clung to him, the worry in her
eye. Even his favorite banana nut muffin couldn't
keep his mind from wandering to her.

Which was why he'd decided checking in on her
was better than trying to ignore how he felt. Instead
of popping in on her unannounced, he'd texted to
see if he could stop by and drop off the folder of information he'd gathered on the history of the manor.

He could have just as easily emailed the information and waited for her to text back for him to do just that, but instead she'd replied *okay* with a thumbs-up emoji. Obviously, she wasn't going to save him from this protective impulse. He wanted to believe maybe she wanted to see him as well, but he was no longer making assumptions when it came to Cierra and her feelings.

She opened the door a few minutes later, wearing the same tank top and shorts she'd had on earlier. "Oh, it's you. Hey, Wes." Her voice was pleasant enough, but the greeting made his stomach drop.

"I texted that I was coming by."

She nodded before waving him in. "I know. I'm sorry. I didn't mean it like that. Troy is supposed to be back with Aria by now and I thought maybe you were him."

Wesley fought not to grimace at the mention of Troy's name. He shouldn't still feel resentment toward Troy. Not after all these years. Honestly, he hadn't thought about Troy or how his former best friend had swooped in and stolen the girl Wesley liked right from under his nose in years. Only when he ran into someone from high school did he remember the way Cierra pulled him aside after that basketball game to tell him that she wasn't really interested in going to prom with him. That she liked someone else and hoped he would be okay with her canceling. The next day, Troy walked her to chemistry class, his arm around her shoulder and a shit-eating grin on his face as everyone oohed and aahed over their high school's newest "it" couple.

When he'd asked Troy how he and Cierra had ended up together, Troy said Cierra had admitted that she'd always liked him. Wesley had been too embarrassed to ask Cierra later why she would ask him then cancel going to prom with him. Not when he already knew the answer. He'd been her way of getting closer to the guy she really liked.

"Is now a bad time?" he asked. He'd rather leave than come face-to-face with his former friend.

She shook her head, reached out, took his wrist in her hand and pulled him forward. "No, come on in. You said you had some history on the house."

Wesley followed her inside. Her home was just as sunny as her personality. The walls were painted a soft yellow color, her furniture all modern earth tones that made the place welcoming, and school pictures of Aria along with group family pictures in frames on every surface and on the walls. He immediately liked it.

"I did, but it's preliminary. I'm going to do some digging at the county museum over the weekend." He pulled out the folder with what he'd pulled together from the messenger bag on his shoulder. "I'll let you know what I find."

She took the folder and looked at the paperwork inside. "Thanks so much, Wesley. I really appreciate you taking the time to help me with this."

"It's what I do."

She glanced up and gave him that sunny smile that made his breathing stutter. "Still, you didn't have to do it for me. Do you want something to drink? I was just about to pour a glass of wine."

"Um...yeah, wine is cool."

She pointed toward the sofa. "Have a seat. I'll be right back."

She turned and went into the kitchen. Wesley stared at her couch and slapped his forehead. What was he thinking? Staying? Having wine? He was only coming to drop off information and make sure she was okay. Not hanging out. She seemed fine. Not only that, *Troy* was coming over. He needed to get the hell up out of there and go home.

He turned toward the kitchen to tell her never mind, but there she was. Coming back out with two wineglasses in her hand.

"Wow, that was fast," he said.

She handed him a glass. "I told you I was about to have a glass. Everything was out." She settled on the sofa. "Have a seat."

He hesitated a second before gingerly sitting on the edge of the sofa. "I didn't mean to impose or anything."

She waved a hand. "You're not imposing. If anything, I'm glad to have someone here. It's part of the reason I'm so anxious to have Aria back home."

His earlier worry returned. "Are you okay? You seemed unsettled when we parted earlier."

She let out a heavy breath. "I was unsettled. I've always kind of believed in ghosts, but I've never really searched them out, much less tried to communicate with one. Today was a lot." She took a sip of her wine.

"The first time can be."

"How do you do it? How do you expose yourself to that all the time?"

He shrugged, sipped his wine. It was a sweet white wine that reminded him of berries. "I don't know. I'm used to it, I guess. When we were younger, we thought it was just cool to go out and find stuff. As we got older and decided to do a little more digging, I became interested in the stories we'd find out. Now, I'm not really scared."

She narrowed her eyes. "You're never scared."

He laughed and held up a finger. "I said not really scared. I didn't say never scared. Some places can be suspect."

"What's the scariest place you've been?"

"You really want to talk about this? I mean, I don't want to spook you even more."

She nodded and leaned toward him. "I'm interested. And I'm not really spooked when you're with me."

He didn't explore how much those words made

him feel like some kind of damn hero. He took another sip of his drink before telling her the story. From there her interest grew and he relaxed back into the couch as he told her more stories about the adventures he had with his brothers. Before he knew it, she'd refilled both their glasses, which they finished, and they were sitting closer to each other on the couch as they talked. She looked at him as if he were the most interesting man in the world. He wasn't used to being looked at like that. His brothers got all the attention. Dion for being the older, more reliable one. Tyrone for being the young, cute, personable one. Everyone just took Wesley as part of the Livingston brothers package deal.

Not Cierra. Cierra always looked at him as if he were the best part of the package. The treasure inside that she couldn't wait to unwrap.

"Oh my God, Wesley, you're just as cool now as you were back in high school," she said with a crooked grin. "No, I think you're actually cooler."

Her elbow was propped against the back of the couch and her head rested in her hand. She'd pulled her hair out of the ponytail she'd worn earlier sometime between the first and second glass of wine, and her thick hair hung in loose waves around her face to her shoulders. Shoulders that were bare thanks to that tempting tank top she wore. A tank top that despite being loose still managed to cling to her full breasts and hint at the cleavage beneath.

Wesley looked away from her to the empty glass in his hand. He put it on the coffee table. No more of that. He was already drunk on Cierra's presence. "I'm not cool. I just have a cool job."

She scoffed. "There you go trying to play it off. Yes, your job is cool, but so are you. You not only investigate this stuff but you're in tune with emotions and stuff. You're so good at reading people and their feelings. It's one of the things I liked about you."

He raised a brow. "That must have been all you liked about me."

"No…there was a lot I liked about you."

Her wistful tone of voice caught his attention. His eyes met hers. Was it the wine? It had to be the wine, because he could have sworn he saw a flash of interest in her brown eyes. Wesley's heart jackhammered his rib cage as he sat there frozen by a rush of longing he wasn't prepared for.

"There was a lot I liked about you, too, Cierra." The words, low and so terribly honest, came out before he could stop himself.

Her eyes widened a fraction, and this time he wasn't unsure. There was definitely interest in her gaze. The air between them hummed and his body heated as if the temperature in the room had increased by a hundred degrees.

"Like what?" Her voice was as soft as his. Playful, almost flirty.

He was going to blame the wine tomorrow. That had to be what had loosened his lips, because he didn't even think about not answering. "Your smile. The way the light reflected off your hair. The way you always smelled sweet, like flowers. How you would grab my hand and squeeze whenever you got excited about something."

Her hand dropped to his resting on the cushion between them. "Like this?" She gave the slightest bit of pressure.

Desire shot straight from where he touched him to his dick. His stomach contracted and he sucked in a breath. "Exactly like that."

He didn't know who moved first, but they both leaned in and the next thing he knew his mouth was on hers and damn did she taste sweet. Her lips, soft and luscious, opened against his and she let out the softest of sighs before her hand curled tighter around his.

Chapter Ten

The heat of Wesley's body lured Cierra to press closer. She couldn't believe he'd kissed her. Not only had he kissed her, but his mouth was a heavenly gift that made her want to crawl into his lap, slide her hands beneath his shirt to the strong muscles beneath and caress every inch of his body. Heat rushed through her veins as his tongue explored her mouth with slow, deliberate strokes.

She leaned into him, and he pulled back. For a second, she worried he was pulling away, but his hand beneath her palm switched so his fingers encircled her wrist and he brought her with him. He settled against the arm of the couch, and she stretched out over his long, lean body. One of his hands explored her back and cupped her ass while the other cradled the back of her head. Cierra's fingers ran across his cheeks and jaw. The roughness of his late-evening stubble sent exciting tingles from her fingers, up her arms to the tips of her breasts.

The last time Cierra had been kissed like this was so long ago she couldn't remember it. She'd forgotten how good it felt to be held, caressed, cherished as if she were something special. Her body rolled against his so she could feel the hard lines of his against the softness of hers. In the back of her mind she wondered how they'd got here, what this meant, if doing this was a bad idea. But when a low groan rumbled through Wesley's chest and his hand squeezed her ass as he held her against him hard enough for the thick press of his erection to dig into her lower belly, she was ready to strip him naked right there on the couch.

Her hand slid down his chest, which rose and fell with his heavy breaths, across his stomach, which caved in with her touch, to the waistband of his pants. Her fingers brushed the button when the doorbell rang. Cierra's head jerked up. She narrowed her eyes toward the door.

"Was that…" She listened for something. She could be wrong. The way the blood rushed in her head she could have been hearing the bells of heaven ringing.

"The doorbell," Wesley said in a low, rumbling voice.

The doorbell chimed again. This time several times. *Aria!* She was back. Not only Aria but… "Crap, it's Troy," Cierra muttered.

She scrambled to get off Wesley. A difficult task considering the way their arms and legs were entangled. Her hand pushed into his stomach as she tried to raise up. He grunted and grimaced.

"Sorry," she said as she moved her hand so she wouldn't crush his diaphragm. Her knee shifted.

"Hold up." Wesley shot up to avoid her knee colliding with his erection. The sudden movement pushed her off him and Cierra tumbled onto the floor. Wesley cursed. "My bad. I didn't mean to do that."

Cierra groaned and quickly jumped up from the floor. "I'm beginning to think you like tossing me out of your lap."

The bell rang again. Cierra didn't look at Wesley and rushed to the front door. She tried to smooth her hair down and wiped her mouth on the way. The movements didn't do a thing. The full, tingling feeling in her lips remained. Her heart pumped quickly, her nipples were tight and her sex throbbed. She took several deep breaths to try to calm down.

She snatched open the door with a bright smile pasted on her face. Aria stood on the porch with Troy behind her. "Hey, baby, I wondered when you'd get home." She opened the screen and took Aria's hand in hers.

"Daddy took me to get white spaghetti and breadsticks," Aria said with a huge grin.

Cierra laughed and nodded. "Oh really. I didn't know you were stopping for food." She glanced up at Troy.

Troy shrugged and gave her his patented it's-not-a-big-deal look. It wouldn't be a big deal if he kept her in the loop. "She loves alfredo and was hungry. I figured it wouldn't hurt."

He lifted his lips in a smile that once, a long time ago, made her feel she could trust him. Now it just reminded her that there were lies behind that smile. Troy was handsome, tall with pecan-brown skin and deep dimples he used to his advantage when dealing with women. She never had proof or reason to suspect infidelity was among Troy's list of wrongs against her, but he'd always insisted he needed to flirt as part of his job as a salesmen. His flirting worked, because there were plenty of women who tried to snatch him away. He'd always been so eager to tell her whenever a woman propositioned him so she would know how lucky she was to have a man who didn't cheat.

Typically, she'd remind him to let her know when he was changing the schedule or time he'd bring Aria home, but she didn't want to get into that right now. She just wanted him gone. "Thanks for getting her dinner."

"Mr. Wesley!" Aria screamed with delight. She rushed into the house and toward Wesley in the living room. "Did you bring more cinnamon rolls?"

Troy's brows drew together. "Mr. Who?"

Wesley cleared his throat and rubbed the back

of his neck as Aria jumped up and down in front of him. "Not today."

"Will you bring some next time?" Aria asked.

"Um...yeah. I'll try to remember."

Troy stepped into the house and glared in the direction Aria had run. He caught one look at Wesley and turned back to Cierra. "You had a man up in here?"

"It's not like that," she said in a low voice. "Wesley is working with me on something."

Troy's eyes traveled over her body. The disheveled clothes and hair. She crossed her arms over her chest when his eyes narrowed on her breasts. Yeah, her nipples were still hard.

"I bet he's working with you," Troy said with a twist of his lips.

Wesley looked toward them. He met Troy's eyes and straightened his shoulders. "What's up, Troy? Long time no see."

Troy glared back. "You got that right. What are you doing here?"

Wesley shrugged in that unapologetic, unfazed way of his. "Just helping Cierra with one of her houses. I dropped off some stuff. I'm going to head out now."

Aria grinned up at Wesley. "But don't forget the cinnamon rolls next time."

Wesley smiled at her and patted her head. "Sure." He crossed over to Cierra and Troy. "Cierra, I'll give you a call this weekend after I finish digging. I'll let you know what I find."

She nodded. "Sure. I appreciate that."

He glanced at Troy, who continued to glare. "Good seeing you, Troy."

Troy didn't respond. Wesley walked out the door without another word. Cierra moved to push the door closed. Wesley paused on the porch and looked back at her. His eyes were a mixture of emotions, but the passion blazing in his eyes sucked the air from her lungs. The corner of his lip lifted in a slight smile. Cierra's own mouth turned up and a soft glow surrounded her heart. He nodded before going down the stairs.

When she closed the door and turned back, her happy feelings were washed away by the scowl on Troy's face. Cierra barely stopped herself from rolling her eyes.

He opened his mouth, but she held up a hand. She looked toward their daughter. "Aria, baby, go and get in the shower, okay. I'll be in there to check on you in a second."

Aria nodded. "Okay, Mommy. Bye, Daddy!"

Troy threw up a hand but didn't look Aria's way. Thankfully, Aria was in such a good mood she didn't notice her dad's slight. She rushed down the hall toward her room. The second her footsteps faded Troy pointed to the door.

"What the hell is he doing here?"

Sighing and crossing her arms she glared at Troy. "I told you what, and why do you care?"

"Because you've got another man up in this house."

"What do you mean *another* man? There isn't a man who currently lives here, pays bills here, or has anything to do with what I do and don't do in this house."

Troy's eyes narrowed. Frustration filled his face. "You know what I mean."

"I don't know what you mean, nor do I care. What I do on my time is my business, Troy. Remember that and stay out of it."

"You can't just have men around my daughter."

She cocked a brow. "Oh really. So when were you going to tell me about Tia?" His eyes widened and his jaw dropped. She held up a hand before he could sputter a lie. "You really think Aria wouldn't tell me about the *special friend* you introduced her to? You want to pull this card, then I can, too."

Troy huffed and then put his hands on his hips. "Look, I was going to tell you about Tia."

"When? Before or after you tried to once again tell me that I should come home and give us another chance? Look, Troy, you mind your business and I'll mind mine, okay?"

The look in his eyes switched from frustration to calculation. She was used to that look; he'd lost the advantage with one argument and had decided to try another angle. "You're going to try with Wesley Livingston again?" he said, disbelief thick in his voice. "I mean, come on, Cierra, I thought you were better than that. He wasn't interested in you back then. In fact, he's probably only messing around with you now to get back at you for being with me."

Cierra groaned and waved away his words. He was giving her a headache. "Goodbye, Troy." She opened the door, grabbed his arm and pulled him toward the door.

"For real. Don't be dumb, Cierra. Don't fall for that guy again."

"I'm not talking to you, Troy." She shoved him out and slammed the door in his face before he could say anything else. She flipped the dead bolt for good measure.

Pressing a hand to her temple, she tried to shove out Troy's words. She knew he was being petty. He wanted to play off her old insecurities. She should ignore him, but the words settled into her brain and spread like a disease through her self-confidence. She had no idea what that kiss meant. What Wesley meant when he said he'd liked a lot about her back then. It could all mean nothing. In the scheme of things his words did mean nothing. The past was the past, and it couldn't be changed. She'd married Troy and was now an entirely different person than the one he'd known then.

That last lingering look he'd given her over his

shoulder, so hot and filled with promise, filled her head. She closed her eyes and shivered. If she weren't careful, she would get lost in fantasies about Wesley. Fantasies that might also have her embarrassed and hurt just as she'd been when they were younger. Until she was a hundred percent sure his kiss meant something more than him trying to scratch a decade-old itch he was suddenly given the opportunity to scratch, she would guard her heart against Wesley Livingston.

Chapter Eleven

Cierra handed a flyer for the Literacy Council's upcoming prom to a woman and smiled. "I hope you can make it."

The woman smiled and nodded before drifting off into the crowd along Main Street. Cierra glanced at Cetris, also manning the Literacy Council's table at the Saturday farmer's market. Cetris pursed her lips and glanced at the woman's departing back.

"She only stopped to get one of those bottles of hand sanitizer," Cetris said.

Cierra shrugged and glanced at the small bottles of sanitizer emblazoned with the council's logo laid out on the table next to the various flyers for activities and postcards about books written by some of the authors the council supported in the past. "At least the hand sanitizer is making people stop. You have to admit their table isn't the most exciting."

Cetris chuckled. "That's for sure."

They'd agreed to "man" the table at the farmer's market for a few hours while their mom and the rest of the council members hosted a book signing with several local authors at the library. The Literacy Council was one of the various clubs and organizations her mom was involved in, and she served as its president. Olivia had completed four years of college and a year of law school when she'd married their father. She'd stepped back to support his law practice, and after she'd had Cierra she'd opted to remain at home as a stay-at-home wife and mother. After Cierra and Cetris graduated high school, Olivia filled her time volunteering after their dad insisted it was too late for her to try to get back in the legal field.

Her mother said she never regretted the decision and all she'd ever really wanted was to be there for her husband and kids. Cierra believed her mother's decision was part of the reason why she couldn't fathom Cierra leaving Troy and striking out on her own instead of staying and making things work to keep her family together.

Cetris slid closer to Cierra. "Okay, what happened next?"

Cierra stopped straightening the flyers on the table and glanced at her sister. "Nothing. Troy acted like I was being dumb as hell for having Wesley over and I kicked him out."

Cetris raised her brows. "Did he catch you two kissing?"

"No. Thank God the door was locked. Otherwise, him and Aria would have got an eyeful of us on the couch."

Cetris's eyes widened, and she slapped Cierra on the shoulder. "What! Y'all were laid out on the couch?"

"I mean…we were sitting there talking and then the kiss just kind of happened. I wasn't planning for anything like that. I'm kind of glad Troy and Aria came home when they did. Otherwise…"

Cetris slapped her shoulder again. "You wouldn't have."

Someone walking over to the table kept Cierra from answering. She handed the man a flyer and a bottle of hand sanitizer while hoping he would stick around and ask a few questions. She'd told Cetris the story because she needed to talk it out. What did the kiss mean and what should she do next? But now that she'd put it out there, she was afraid to explore the meaning. As much as she hated to admit it, Troy's words had stuck to her like old chewing gum. She wished she could scrape them off and just go with what she wanted. Instead, every time she thought of the pleasure she'd felt from Wesley's kiss, she also felt the sticky, uncomfortable mess of Troy's words.

The guy took the handout and bottle, then walked away. Leaving Cierra with no choice but to continue the conversation.

"So…answer me," Cetris said as soon as he walked off. "Would you?"

Cierra lifted a shoulder and avoided her sister's eye. "I don't know. Maybe."

"For real?"

"The guy can kiss and I am so…" She searched for the right words.

Cetris bumped her shoulder against Cierra's. "Horny?"

Cierra pushed her sister away and laughed. "No!" Cetris twisted her lips and gave her a *whatever* look. Cierra shrugged. "Okay…yeah, but that's not why. I have a Danny the Dildo, and if I just wanted sex, I could find a guy to sleep with. It was the way he kissed me. The way he touched me. Like I was special. I don't know, Cetris, I liked that feeling. I miss feeling that way."

Cetris's eyes turned pensive. "Be careful with that. I get that you used to like Wesley and he can be a decent guy, but don't mix up lust with something else. You say he touched you like you were special. Could that be because Troy groped at you like you were his handy sex object for so long?"

Cierra sighed. "I don't want to believe that's the case."

"Not wanting to believe it doesn't make it less true. You told me yourself there was no intimacy between you and Troy. Don't get confused because Wesley is the first guy you've got close to having sex with since your divorce."

"But I think he felt something, too."

"Maybe he did, but you thought he felt something in high school, too."

Cetris's words struck a nerve. A few people came over to their table and they gave the usual update about the Literacy Council and the upcoming prom. Many people were excited about the idea of the adult prom fundraiser. Mrs. Montgomery had been right about giving adults a reason to get dressed up for a fun and exciting event. After a few minutes of Cierra and Cetris handing out items, the crowd thinned again.

Cetris turned to her. "Okay, who kissed who first?"

"Why does that matter?"

"Because you're sitting over there with sad puppy dog eyes after what I said. If he kissed you first, then maybe he likes you, too."

Cierra thought about how the kiss started. "I don't know. It seems like it happened at the same time. But…maybe I leaned in first." She rubbed her eyes and tried to remember.

Cetris put a hand on her shoulder. "You know what? It doesn't matter. Just ask the guy straight up. Find out what he wants. If he says it was a mistake, then you know it's time to move on. If he wants to kiss you again, then you have to figure out if he wants to make you a consistent booty call or just to hit a few times and move on."

Cierra rubbed the back of her neck. "Ugh, I am not supposed to be living this life. I was supposed to stay married."

"Troy will take you back in a hot minute," Cetris said, studying her nails.

Cierra shivered. "Hell no. You know what I mean."

She wasn't ready for the uncertainty of dating. As much as she didn't want to go back to Troy, she also couldn't deny that she missed the stability of not having to figure out the hidden meanings behind words and kisses. She'd figured out Troy and knew he was full of crap. The thought of Wesley being the same made her skin itch and her heart stutter.

She sighed. "I'm not ready to date again."

"Yes, you are. You just have to be smart about it." Cetris glanced around. "The crowd isn't so bad. Walk around. Clear your head. Mom should be back soon and then we can leave."

Cierra took her sister's advice and left the table. She wasn't in the right mood to be entertaining and pleasant anyway. Not with all the thoughts about her and Wesley swirling in her head. He was so much in her thoughts that she imagined seeing him in the crowd. Walking down the street. Hanging out at a vendor. Laughing with a woman at the vendor booth. A woman who put her hand on his arm.

Cierra stopped walking. Her head cocked to the side. That wasn't her imagination. That was Wesley. And he was looking like he was having a fantastic time laughing it up with another woman just a few days after kissing her.

* * *

Wesley smiled and listened while Porcha gave him an update on the latest with her son and the rest of her family. He'd come to the farmer's market specifically to see her. They'd dated for about eighteen months before mutually agreeing to break things off six months ago. They were still friends and got along with no problems even after the breakup. He hadn't planned to go looking for her, but when the historian he planned to meet about the DeWalt Manor canceled on him and he'd been stuck in the house reliving the kiss with Cierra over and over again until he was hard and aching, he knew he had to get out of the house.

Porcha mixed her own spices and sugars and sold them at the farmer's market. Baking always helped him clear his mind and nothing brought out the flavor of the coffee cake he planned to make better than her mocha-infused sugar. Six months of separation meant he'd forgotten about all of the drama in Porcha's family and the way she loved to give him full detailed accounts of everything going on.

Porcha placed a hand on his arm and leaned in. "Can you believe Cory and his cousins tried to coerce me and my cousin Linda to take them to the skating rink? It was a whole mess."

She laughed and Wesley half-heartedly laughed along with her. He glanced at the container of mocha sugar sitting on her table. The container he'd waited over ten minutes for her to charge him for but instead had to sit through her detailed family update. "Well, you know, I guess they really wanted to go."

"I know, but they could've just asked. They didn't have to make up some elaborate story about why they needed to go."

"But would you have taken them if they'd asked?"

"Probably not," she said with a grin.

Her hand remained on his arm and her fingers tightened in a light squeeze. She'd moved closer to him, and the fruity smell of her body spray drifted up to him. He used to like her fruity smell and the way she'd squeeze his arm. Once, both would make him think about pulling her close or getting her alone later. Today, he felt none of that. She was still just as attractive. Same dimples, same honey-gold skin, same neat blond dreads. But his mind was preoccupied with another woman.

"What are you doing later today?" she asked. "If you're not busy, maybe you could come by. I know Cory would like to see you."

He also knew that look in her eye. Apparently she also remembered the way he used to react to her. "Um...I don't know if that's the best idea."

"Why not? Are you seeing someone?"

The word *no* formed on his lips but wouldn't come out of his mouth. What was wrong with him? He wasn't seeing anyone. He'd only kissed Cierra. That didn't mean they were dating or anything. That didn't stop the thought of saying he wasn't single from making his stomach twist in knots.

"Wesley? What are you doing here?"

Wesley's entire body froze. Had the constant fantasies of their kiss conjured her up? His head spun in the direction of her voice and his heart jumped in his throat. Cierra watched him with suspicious eyes. Her gaze dropped to where Porcha still touched his arm, to Porcha, and then to him. Wesley stepped aside until Porcha's hand fell away.

"Hey, Cierra." His face burned and he tried to figure out why he felt guilty. He wasn't guilty. He hadn't done anything wrong.

"I thought you were researching today?" There was no accusation in her voice, but he saw the sentiment in the depths of her brown eyes.

"Let me ring this up." Porcha turned away quickly and reached for her phone with the credit card reader inserted into the outlet slot.

Now she wanted to hurry this transaction along! Wesley pulled out his wallet to get his credit card. "I was gonna call you," he said to Cierra. "The historian canceled on me today. I'm going to meet up with him next weekend instead."

He handed his card to Porcha. She took it and smirked. "Still using this beat-up card. I told you to replace it."

"It doesn't expire for another six months," he said automatically.

"You always were stubborn," she replied with a wink and a smile.

Cierra ran a hand through her hair and glanced away. "Okay, well, I'll talk to you later, then."

She turned and walked away without a word. Porcha took her time swiping and running his card. Wesley looked from her slow card scanner to Cierra's quickly retreating back.

"I guess you are seeing someone," Porcha said, handing him back his card.

"It's not like that." He took the card and shoved it into his wallet.

"So, I guess you aren't about to chase her down and further explain why you're not where she thought you'd be?" A sly grin creased her face and she handed him the bag with his sugar.

He glared at her, and she only continued to grin. "Bye, Porcha." He took the bag and hurried off after Cierra with Porcha's laugh following him.

He maneuvered through the crowd. His eyes trained on the bright orange T-shirt she'd been wearing. Despite the crowd, it didn't take long for him to reach her, and he put his hand on her elbow to stop her. Cierra swung around, eyes wide and hand half raised as if she were ready to hit him. She let out a breath and put the same hand she'd raised over her heart.

"You scared me," she said in a rush.

"My bad."

"Why did you grab me?"

"I didn't grab you. I touched your elbow to get your attention. I wanted to talk to you."

She crossed her arms and raised a brow. "About what?"

"About..." He hesitated. Why did he feel the need to explain himself? He shouldn't have to explain himself. They weren't together, but then there was that kiss. A kiss that made him think about her night and day and had him considering what would it take to kiss her again.

"Wesley?" she asked with a raised brow.

"Sorry I didn't get the chance to call you about having to cancel with the historian today. I was going to, but then I..." The words stuck in his throat again. I couldn't get the kiss out of my mind, and I knew if I called you, then I'd try to find a way to see you again.

"You decided to come to the farmer's market and flirt instead," she said.

"Yes... I mean, no. I came because I knew Porcha would be here. She has a sugar blend I need for the cake I'm making later today."

"Oh, so you came for Porcha's sugar," she said with a twist of her lips.

"So I can make a cake. A cake I hoped to share with you. If you were okay with that." The words came out without him thinking about them, but he didn't regret saying them. He hadn't thought things through, but he knew that baking something was another reason for him to see her again. He had promised Aria something sweet.

Her mouth formed a cute O shape and the stiffness in her shoulders lessened as she slowly uncrossed her arms. "I mean, I would've been okay with that."

His heart soared and the edges of his lips lifted in what he knew had to be a goofy-ass grin. He was losing the battle to not fall for Cierra again.

"Cierra, what are you doing over here and not at the table?" A woman's voice cut into the moment.

They both turned as Cierra's mother rushed over to them. Olivia glanced at him and smiled. "Hi, Wesley. Congratulations on the show." She turned to Cierra before he could respond. "Did you leave your sister at the table?"

"I'm on my way back there now."

Her mom nodded. "Did you give out most of the flyers? We're trying to get a good turnout." She spun back to Wesley. "The Literacy Council is hosting an adult prom in a few weeks. You're coming, aren't you?"

Wesley gaped for a second. "Um…I don't know." He hadn't given the prom a second thought after Mrs. Montgomery mentioned it at the furniture store the other day.

She pinched Cierra's arm. "You didn't tell him?"

Cierra pushed her mom's hand away and rubbed

her arm. "We just ran into each other. And Mrs. Montgomery already told him."

"Well, you've got to come. We're raising money for the library expansion. Maybe you can take Cierra." She grinned and looked expectantly between Wesley and Cierra.

His gaze met Cierra's. The awkwardness of the last time they were supposed to go to the prom zipped between them. They were no longer kids. It wasn't like he'd ask her now and she'd dump him for Troy again, but still he froze. He was transported back to the teenage boy who'd been crazy about Cierra, only to have her drop him without a second thought. All because of a kiss he wasn't sure meant anything other than they were attracted to each other and had acted on it after two glasses of wine.

Cierra put her hands on her mom's shoulders. "Okay, that's enough, Mom. Let's go back to the table. See you later, Wesley."

She turned her mom away and started down the street.

"Cierra," he called. When she turned back to him, he spoke before he chickened out. He may feel like that embarrassed kid, but he wasn't anymore. He wanted to see her again, kiss her again, and figure out what was going on in her heart and mind before someone else did. "I'll drop off the cake later. If that's okay."

She gave a small, sweet smile before nodding and guiding her mom farther down the street. Wesley didn't fight his grin as he watched her walk away.

Chapter Twelve

Cierra got Aria settled in the middle of the living room floor with her notebook of drawing paper and a multitude of markers and colored pencils when the doorbell rang. Her heart almost lurched out of her chest. She dropped the box of markers in her hand and spun toward the door.

"Who is it?" Aria said in a singsong voice. Something she sometimes did when the doorbell rang.

"Let's see, baby," Cierra said, giving her usual response.

She wiped her sweaty palms on the lounge pants she'd changed into after showering and went to the door. It could be anyone. Cetris might've decided to show up and hang out with her older sister and niece versus going out for drinks with friends after a day at the farmer's market. Though she'd mostly broken him of the habit, Troy might suddenly decide to pop up. It could even be her neighbor across the street, Pat, coming to tell her that she'd left the garage door up.

Deep in her heart she didn't believe it was any of

those people. She'd wondered if Wesley would really show up with a cake he'd baked with the sugar he'd purchased from the woman who felt comfortable enough to put her hand on his arm. The woman who knew what type of credit card he kept in his wallet. She didn't want to be jealous, but the man had kissed her senseless. She had a right to wonder why he was flirting with another woman so soon after.

She checked the peephole and her racing heart did a backflip. Wesley stood on her porch with what looked like a cake in his hands. He'd really baked for her. The gesture was small and sweet, and a warm glow surrounded her heart.

She took a deep breath, smoothed her hair, then opened the door. Wesley stilled in the middle of shifting his weight from foot to foot. His dark eyes traveled from her head to her feet and back up. She would've wished she'd chosen something cuter to change into once she'd came home and showered off the sweat and tiredness of working the Literacy Council table, but the glow of appreciation in Wesley's eyes chased away that thought.

"You came," she said.

He let out a low chuckle. "You always say that as if I'm not going to follow through."

"I wasn't sure if you'd make it by. No big plans for a Saturday night?" she asked casually, when she really wanted to know if he'd made plans to hang out with the woman from the farmer's market.

"I do have big plans." He held up the cake. "To bring you this."

She almost gushed but caught herself before she did. She stepped back. "Come on in."

He crossed the threshold and followed her farther into the house. Aria looked up from her drawings and beamed. "Mr. Wesley, did you bring cinnamon rolls?" She popped up from the floor and ran toward him.

Wesley chuckled. "I did one better. I made a cake. I hope you like it."

Aria jumped up and tried to get a good look at the cake in Cierra's hands. "A birthday cake?"

"Not a birthday cake. It's a coffee cake."

Her face scrunched up. "I can't drink coffee."

"That's just what it's called. No coffee is in it."

She grinned at Cierra. "Does that mean I can have some?"

Cierra nodded. "Yes. Let me cut this and we'll all give it a try."

Aria clapped her hands then grabbed Wesley's hand. "Wanna see my pictures? My auntie says I'm an artist."

Wesley pointed to the papers on the floor. "Did you draw some of these?"

"I did. Sit down and see."

She tugged Wesley down to the floor. Cierra left them there and went into the kitchen to slice the cake. If it tasted as good as it smelled, then she had no doubt she and Aria would enjoy it. When she came back into the living room a few minutes later, Wesley listened intently while Aria explained what she'd tried to convey in each drawing. The sight of them together sent a strong pull of longing through her midsection.

She shook her head. No, ma'am! She was not about to start having visions of her, Aria and Wesley as a happy family. They weren't even dating, and furthermore, she still didn't have answers about him and that woman from earlier. A woman he obviously had history with. Not to mention that after ten years unhappily married, Cierra wasn't ready to sign up for another long-term relationship, much less marriage.

"Here's the cake," she said.

"Yay," Aria said and reached for her slice.

Cierra handed a slice first to Aria then Wesley before sitting on the floor with them with hers. Wesley watched them anxiously as they took their first bites. The cake was sweet and flavorful. Both she and Aria nodded their approval. He relaxed and took a bite.

"How did you learn how to bake cakes?" Aria asked.

"I used to bake with my mom when I was little. She always made our birthday cakes, or she'd get up on the weekend to make brownies or cookies. It was fun."

"Does she still make cookies and cakes?" Aria asked, sounding hopeful.

Wesley shook his head and gave a sad smile. "Not anymore. My mom passed away a long time ago."

Aria froze and gave Cierra a worried look. Cierra patted her hair and gave her a reassuring smile. She hadn't expected Aria to go there with the questioning. Her daughter was naturally curious and liked to understand things, so Cierra encouraged her to ask questions. She hoped Wesley wasn't angry with the quick turn of topic.

"It's okay to ask," Wesley said, noticing her discomfort. "I don't mind talking about my mom and dad."

Aria stood and gave Wesley a hug. When she straightened, she patted his head. "You make really good cakes. I bet your mom did, too."

Wesley nodded. "She did."

"Mommy doesn't make cakes. She buys them, but maybe one day you can show me how to make them?"

Wesley glanced at Cierra. "If your mom is okay with that. Maybe one day." Surprisingly, there wasn't a panicked look in his eye. She couldn't quite read his expression, but her longing from earlier tried to make a comeback.

Heat prickled Cierra's cheeks and she had to bite the corner of her mouth to keep from grinning like a fool. She was getting way ahead of herself with these feelings toward Wesley and she needed to get them under control before she found herself embarrassed, stumbling into a relationship that she later regretted.

"Um…we'll see."

"Yay!" Aria clapped and pointed to the pictures. "Will you draw with me?"

Cierra waved a hand. "Aria, I'm sure—"

"I can't draw well, but I'll try." Wesley spoke at the same time as her.

That was all Aria needed to hear. She sat down and slid paper and markers in Wesley's direction before finishing her slice of cake. Not wanting to be left out, Cierra decided to draw a picture with them. The entire time Wesley was patient and attentive as Aria explained how he should draw and what colors worked better. When they were done, Aria had a good picture of a unicorn underneath a rainbow, Cierra had drawn something that could pass for a cat, and Wesley had a genuinely nice sketch of a house.

She leaned forward to get a better look. "That's your family home," she said, recognizing the structure.

He nodded. "Yeah, it was the easiest thing I could think to draw."

Aria slid close to him and pointed at the picture. "You said you couldn't draw."

"Well, I can't draw people or animals as good as

you, but I'm pretty good with drawing buildings and houses." When Aria gave him a questioning look, he replied, "I'm an architect so it's kind of my job."

Aria's eyes lit up with interest. "What's an architect?"

"Someone who designs new buildings before they're built."

"Cool!"

"Aria, it's getting close to bedtime," Cierra jumped in. She recognized the look on her daughter's face. Aria was ready to jump in and ask twenty questions, which would lead to twenty more and so on. "Mr. Wesley can answer your questions about his job another time."

Aria sighed but nodded. "Okay. Will you answer them next time?"

Wesley nodded. "I sure will."

Her daughter grinned. "And bring another cake?"

Wesley chuckled. "We'll see. I can't bring you a cake every time I come by."

"Be thankful for the cake he brought today," Cierra said. She stood and helped Aria to her feet. "Go to your room and get ready for bed."

"Okay, Mommy." Aria gave Cierra a hug then waved at Wesley. "Good night, Mr. Wesley."

He waved back. "Good night, Aria."

She grinned at them both then ran toward her room. After Aria left, Cierra and Wesley stared at each other awkwardly for a few seconds. When Aria was there, it was easy to get lost in her daughter's enthusiasm and let her innocent chatter fill the void. Cierra dropped her gaze from him to the couch. Wesley turned in the direction she looked and then cleared his throat.

"Well, I guess I should go," he said.

Cierra ran her hands along her thighs and nodded. "Thank you for stopping by and bringing the cake."

"It was no problem."

Their eyes met and Cierra swallowed hard. The couch was visible in her periphery and a vision of the two of them spread on top of the cushions, Wesley's hands in her hair, their lips pressed together and the hard length of him against her stomach filled her mind. Wesley's eyes narrowed slightly, and his knowing gaze seemed to read exactly where her thoughts had gone.

He leaned toward her, and Cierra's heart imitated a jackrabbit. She couldn't kiss him now. Not here, when Aria could walk in any second. Cierra spun and walked to the door. A heartbeat later Wesley followed her.

Would it be awkward or rude to bring up the woman from earlier? That and the kiss. She didn't like being in limbo and she really didn't want to end up thinking it meant something to her when it didn't mean as much to Wesley. She hated this unsettled feeling. She hadn't dated in years and wasn't sure what the new rules of the game were.

She opened the door and went onto the porch with Wesley. Whatever she was going to say she didn't want to do it in the house with the possibility of Aria overhearing. Her daughter was inquisitive, and she had no filter. Anything she overheard today would be repeated to her parents, Cetris and possibly Troy.

"Are you busy next weekend?"

"Who was that woman earlier?"

They spoke at the same time. Cierra's lips parted on a surprised inhale. Wesley's brows drew together.

"You go first," she said. Her answer to his question was dependent on what he said.

"That's Porcha." He stopped as if that were enough and she raised a brow. "We used to date."

Cierra rubbed the back of her neck. Realistically, she knew he'd dated before. That didn't mean she had to like the idea of seeing his ex-girlfriend groping his arm earlier that day. "Used to. Are you dating now?"

"Would I kiss you like that if I were dating her?"

"I don't know. You tell me." She raised her chin and met his eye. She'd rather hear it from him straight versus playing a word game.

Wesley took a half a step closer and spoke in a deep, decadent voice. "I'm not seeing anyone. I'm free to kiss whomever I want."

His eyes dropped to her lips. Heat slid through Cierra's body. She swallowed hard and fought not to melt into a puddle.

"Oh." Cierra tried not to let how much she wanted him to kiss her senseless right now come through.

"What about you?" he asked. "Are you dating?"

She shook her head. "I'm ready to get back out there after the divorce, but so far there's nothing on the horizon."

He raised a brow. "Nothing?"

Did he mean he was on the horizon? "I mean… no one has said they're interested."

He leaned his head to the side and looked at her as if she were kidding. "A kiss isn't enough to show interest?"

She lifted a shoulder. "I don't know. One kiss might not mean a thing to a guy."

He slid closer until the warmth of his body cushioned her and she had to look up into his eyes. "What about two? Would that be enough?"

Despite telling herself to play it cool, she couldn't stop a grin from spreading across her face. "Two is good, but I think three is the magic number."

He nodded slowly. "Ah, okay. Gotcha." He placed a hand on her hip, eased her against him and lowered his head until their lips met.

This kiss wasn't like the one before. It wasn't as frantic and heat fueled, but it still made her skin tingle and lit a fire in her blood. He kissed her slowly, thoroughly, his lips and tongue tasting her while his arms held her possessively in his embrace. When he broke away much too soon, Cierra grabbed his shirt and pulled him back for another quick, hard kiss.

"Still three?" he asked in a husky voice.

If she doubted his interest before, she didn't now. Everything about Wesley's hot gaze said he wanted her. "Maybe two is good."

His sexy smile made her wish this was Troy's week to have Aria. If that were so, she'd drag him inside, slowly peel of every stitch of clothing he wore and make love to him all night long.

Aria called Cierra's name from inside the house. She stifled a groan. "I should get back inside."

He nodded and let her go. "I'll call you later this week."

She watched him leave before going back inside to help Aria with bath time. She went through the rest of the night automatically and when she fell into bed later, she reached for Danny the Dildo, and lost herself in the memory of Wesley's kiss and the sweet torture of imagining all of the naughty things promised in his smile.

Chapter Thirteen

Wesley missed having his brothers around, but he hadn't realized how much of a hole was left in his life until they rang the doorbell of his condo on Saturday morning. They'd hugged then drank coffee in Wesley's kitchen as they went over their plans for the day: to dig up whatever information they could on the DeWalt Manor. After Wesley updated them on what he'd heard when he'd visited the manor with Cierra, his brothers had both insisted on coming to help him dig up more information. They didn't care about this being for the show. Their excitement over discovering the truth and their love of paranormal investigation fueled their desire.

They agreed that Wesley and Tyrone would meet with the local historian to discuss any stories and legends surrounding the property, while Dion would scour the news records at the library. They would meet up later at the Waffle House to go over what they'd found and eat lunch.

Wesley and Tyrone headed to the county's museum, which was located in a renovated home built in the nineteenth century. The museum was dedicated to preserving the history of Sunshine Beach and the surrounding area. The home was filled with the original furniture of the family who once lived there, along with artifacts and other items donated to the museum by various influential families from Sunshine Beach.

The historian, Dave, was a slim young white man with brown hair and an eager smile. He wore a yellow button-up shirt with brown pants and had set up a table with tea and cookies along with a stack of books in the back corner of the museum.

"I'm sorry about canceling last week," Dave said once they were settled. "I forgot there was a group tour planned for that day."

Wesley shrugged. "It was no problem. I appreciate you taking the time to meet with us."

Tyrone glanced around the museum. "Other people pulled up when we did. Are you sure you'll have time today?"

Dave nodded. "Yes, my part-timer is here today. She can manage without me. On a typical weekend we only get a few people coming through."

Wesley pointed to the stacks of books. "Are these for today?"

Dave's eyes lit up. "Yes. When you first called me, I wasn't sure what I'd have to offer. We have a few items from the house in the museum, but the family kept most of their things in the home for display there. But it's also a good thing I canceled last week, because I was digging around in storage on Wednesday looking for something else when I came across a box of old donations."

"What kind of donations?" Tyrone asked.

"We get all kinds of stuff. People find things their grandparents had and give it to the museum. Unless we see something of value it goes into storage. This box had books and was donated several years ago. I looked through it and lo and behold, it's filled with various records. Sales receipts, order forms and even a few household ledgers. Even better, there were old ledgers from the manor dating back to the nineteenth century!" Dave's voice rose with excitement.

Wesley exchanged a look with Tyrone. The enthusiasm in Dave's voice was mirrored in his brother's gaze. They both turned back to Dave and leaned forward.

"The family donated this to the museum?"

Dave shook his head. "I don't think so. When I checked, it looks like the items were donated by a woman named Sally Rutherford. I don't know how she got them or why she gave them to us, but it turned out to be perfect timing for you."

Dave slid on a pair of white gloves and lifted one of the books. "They're in pretty good condition, considering their age."

"Was there anything interesting in the records?" Wesley asked. He balled his hands into fists in his lap to keep from reaching out and grabbing one of the books. He was ready to dive right in and see what he could find.

Tyrone must have felt the same, because he shifted forward in his seat and leaned closer to try to read what was on the pages Dave uncovered.

"To me, yes. I love seeing a glimpse into everyday life. For you, I'm not sure. Like I said, there isn't much recorded that might help you with your investigation. These records let us know what they typically ordered for groceries and household needs. No real family secrets." Dave looked up from the book and gave them a pensive stare. "The family owned about a hundred people at one time. There's one book with a listing of who was sold or purchased. Sometimes with a name. Sometimes without."

Tyrone's movements stopped. He recoiled from the books as if poisoned and scowled. "That's what's in these records."

Dave nodded slowly. "Not all. Most are from the early- to mid-twentieth century. Only one lists people as…"

"Commodities," Tyrone said in a tight voice.

Wesley squeezed his brother's shoulder. He understood Tyrone's frustration. He felt it, too. The sadness and anger of being confronted with the stark reality of the lives of their ancestors. "This Rutherford woman. Do you know if she's still around? I'm curious to know how she got all this."

Dave's brows drew together as he considered. "I don't know a Sally Rutherford, but I did go to high school with an Alicia Rutherford. She lives over in Cottontown, I believe." Dave referred to a neighborhood in Sunshine Beach.

"That's not much to go on," Tyrone said.

"I know. I wish I had more."

Wesley did, too. He looked back at the books. "Anything other than household ledgers and receipts here?"

Dave shook his head. "Not much. A few notes in the side about amounts and brands, but I don't know if they'll shed any light. What I can tell you is that the DeWalt family was one of the first families to settle the area. They got much of that land thanks to headrights back in the seventeen hundreds."

"You mean when English aristocrats were given land based on the number of people they owned."

"Basically," Dave said. "It wasn't much at first. The family eventually purchased more land over time and expanded. The Civil War bankrupted them and they struggled to keep the place afterward but managed to find a way to keep most of the property. You know the rest of the story of how they monetized it in the eighties and nineties."

"Any stories or legends surrounding the manor?" Wesley asked.

"Just the typical ghost stories." Dave frowned and tapped his chin.

Dave told them a few of the ghost stories he'd heard. Mostly from tourists and visitors who'd been to the place over the years. The same stories Wesley had dug up via an internet search. What struck him as odd was the lack of an origin story. Most places that were haunted had an origin story. A person who died too soon or suddenly with unfinished business. The DeWalt family had nothing. No mention of unexplained or unusual deaths. No explanation whatsoever for the ghost. Just that they suddenly appeared. That didn't sit right with Wesley.

As they left the museum an hour later and got into the car to meet Dion, Wesley shook his head. "Something's not right," he said.

Tyrone frowned as he put on his seat belt. "No… it's not."

"What are you thinking?" he asked.

"That someone's keeping a secret," Tyrone said.

He glanced at his brother. "Are you thinking what I'm thinking."

Tyrone nodded. "Find Sally Rutherford?"

Wesley pointed. "We need to find her and figure out why she had all of the ledgers for the manor. I don't know why, but I've got a feeling Ms. Rutherford may have more of that family's secrets."

After meeting with Dion and comparing notes, the brothers agreed that finding Sally Rutherford was the next step. They didn't have much to go on, so instead of starting a fruitless search that day, they chose to end the investigation for now and spend the following week or so pulling resources to see what they could dig up on the Rutherford family.

When Dion suggested they go back to the family home and hang out for the rest of the night instead of going to Wesley's condo, he agreed. He didn't think about the changes he'd made to the place or the furniture he'd got removed until they opened the front door and his brothers stopped soon after they crossed the threshold and got a look at the empty living room.

The smile on Wesley's face froze the second he noticed the confused and panicked looks on his brother's faces. He'd been so caught up in the investigation and having his brothers around that his plans to sell the house had flown from his mind. He was going to tell them and get their buy in, but he hadn't wanted to reveal that he'd already started the process like this.

"What the hell happened in here?" Dion asked first.

Tyrone rushed to the center of the living room and looked around. "Where's all the furniture?"

Wesley put down the bag containing a six-pack of beers they'd picked up. "The furniture is fine. It's in storage."

Dion spun around toward him. "Storage? Why is it in storage?"

"Because I was going to bring in new furniture."

Tyrone scowled. "You're redecorating the house?"

"Not quite," he answered.

Dion crossed his arms over his chest. "What does that mean? Why did you take the furniture out? Is this the only room?"

Wesley wasn't ready to answer any of those questions, but he decided to go with the easiest of them. "I'm changing a few other rooms, too."

Dion's eyes widened. "What?" He rushed from the empty living room and checked the rest of the downstairs.

Tyrone was right on his heels. Wesley followed slowly behind them. They checked the family and dining rooms before ending in the kitchen. Along the way Dion called out all the things that were missing.

"What the hell, Wes," Dion said. "I'm barely out of the house and you're getting rid of everything."

"You're not barely out of the house," he shot back. "You've been out of the house for nine months and you're not moving back."

"That doesn't mean you can change everything."

Tyrone walked over to Dion and placed a hand on his shoulder. "Hold up. Let's hear the reason. I mean, it's Wes. There's got to be a good damn reason for him to get rid of all of our stuff."

"I didn't get rid of anything," Wesley said evenly despite the pounding of his heart. He wasn't going to cave in on this. For once, his brothers were going to go along with what he wanted. "I put it in storage."

"You gonna tell us why?" Tyrone asked.

Wesley took a deep breath. "I'm staging the house."

Tyrone frowned. "Staging? What the hell is a staging?"

Dion's eyes narrowed. "You better not mean what I think you mean."

Wesley squared his shoulders. Selling the place was the right decision. They were gone and he wasn't going to be left behind to take care of everything just because they hadn't thought of this first. "I think we should sell the place."

Tyrone snatched his hand back. "Sell the house?"

Dion shook his head. "We are not selling the house."

"Why not?" Wesley asked. "You're living in Charlotte now. Tyrone is off gallivanting and doing his own thing."

Tyrone held up a hand. "Hold up, *gallivanting*? What the hell? Who says that?"

"I say it," Wesley said. "Because it's true. Let's face it. You've both moved on. You left me here and told me to take care of the house. Well, this is me taking care of it."

"Nah, this is you going too far," Dion said.

Wesley placed a hand on his chest. "I'm going too far? How?"

Dion looked at Wesley as if he'd grown a third eye. "Because you can't just sell the house."

"I'm not selling the house. I'm getting it prepped for sale."

Tyrone's lip twisted. "How is that any different?"

"Because I know I can't sell without you agreeing. I'm just getting an idea of what the place would go for. I'm working with Cierra to stage the rooms."

Dion blinked and scowled. "Hold up, you already got a Realtor?"

"It's not like that. I'm helping her with the De-Walt Manor and when I mentioned possibly selling the place, she said she'd give me some ideas to help it go for more. That's all I'm doing."

"No." Dion slashed his hand through the hair. "The answer is no. We aren't selling."

Tyrone nodded. "I agree."

Wesley took in the determined set of Dion's jaw, and the way Tyrone crossed his arms and glared at Wesley as if he were a kid who'd disappointed them both. Wesley's shoulders tightened as frustration prickled across his skin. They thought this was the end of it. That they could just command something and Wesley would go along with it like he had when they were younger. Not this time.

Wesley gave them both in incredulous look. "Are either of you coming back here to stay?"

"We aren't selling the house," Dion said.

"See, there's my answer. You don't want to live

here and you're both ready to go on about your business, but you want me to stay here and take care of everything. Did you even think to stop and ask if I wanted to take care of the house? Did you stop to ask what I wanted out of all of this, or did you just decide that you'll leave it to me to handle anything you don't want to handle?"

"What's that supposed to mean?" Tyrone asked.

"It means exactly what I said. All my life I've played peacemaker for you two. I've gone along with whatever I needed to so we could all get along. I kept the house going while you worked, Dion, and Tyrone played around. Now that you've got your own lives, you want me to keep on doing that. Well, I'm not. I've got things I want to do, and it isn't keeping the house clean and dusted for whenever you two suddenly decide to come visit. You don't want to sell the place, then you come home and take care of it." He turned and marched out of the front door before they could say anything else.

Chapter Fourteen

Cierra waited exactly forty-eight hours for Wesley to give her an update on what he and his brothers had learned when they'd investigated the manor's history. She hadn't expected him to contact her immediately. Not when he hadn't spent time with his brothers in so long and she knew he was looking forward to hanging with them. That's why after the first day passed with no updates she hadn't thought much of it. The second day, when she'd texted him to see how things were going and she'd got no answer, she'd also attributed that to him being busy and let it slide. Now, after texting, again, and getting no answer she was starting to worry.

Other than when he hadn't responded when she'd initially tried to get in contact with him, he was good about answering calls and texts. She didn't want to go off the deep end and think something was wrong, but she had a lot riding on the sale of the manor and his sudden silence was making her nervous. She'd taken a woman to lunch the day before who'd recently received her real estate license and the mention of the manor had the woman interested in joining Cierra's company. If that fell through, she'd not only lose hiring a potential agent to work for her, but run the risk of people in the industry saying she was unreliable or worse: a liar.

She grabbed her cell phone off her desk and called him. If he didn't answer, she'd do a reconnaissance mission and track him down like she'd done before. After five rings, she was beginning to think she'd have to track him down when he finally answered.

"Cierra, hey, I've been meaning to call you." His voice was a little breathless and rushed.

Cierra frowned. "Is everything okay?"

"Yeah, it's just been a busy day. I've got a request for a new project and I'm finishing up another design. Are you in your office? I was going to drop by if you had time. I need to talk to you about a few things."

"I'm here. What time were you coming by?"

"I'll be there in a few minutes. I came out to grab lunch and it'll be easier to swing by than come out later. That cool?"

"Works for me. See you in a bit."

The call ended and she stared at her phone. He didn't sound like anything was wrong, but if there wasn't a problem, why would he need to come by and see her in person? What had he found out that he couldn't tell her over the phone? Had he found out something that would make selling the DeWalt Manor next to impossible?

She cringed and pressed a hand to her temple. She really hoped not. Not only did she have a potential new agent to work for her, she'd recently sent gifts to her former clients thanking them for working with her and asking them to refer her to any family or friends who may need a Realtor. A few phone calls resulted from that, and she was grateful for any new leads. She could hopefully make a decent profit if she sold another house or two this year, but selling the manor would be a comfortable cushion going into the next year.

Wesley arrived after a few minutes. He walked into her office and Cierra immediately felt as if the space was too small. He was dressed casually in a pair of camel-colored slacks and a short-sleeved white polo. Wesley was tall and he wasn't overly broad or heavily muscled, but there was strength in the long, lean lines of his body. Strength she'd felt as she'd stretched on top of him on the couch and when he'd pulled her into his embrace for a kiss. Strength she hadn't realized how much she wanted to feel against her body again until he stood in front of her.

"I hope I didn't catch you at a bad time," he said.

She shook her head and stood from her desk. "Not a bad time at all. Do you want anything to drink?"

He shook his head and pointed to the couch. "Nah, I'm good. Let's sit over here."

She tried not to let her anxiety kick up, but his serious expression wasn't making things easier. She crossed the room and sat next to him. "What's wrong?"

He ran his hands over his pants and took a deep breath. "I'm not sure if I can sell the house."

"The manor?"

He shook his head. "No. My house. The family house. I'm not sure if I should sell it."

She relaxed and understanding dawned. "Is that why you haven't returned my texts? You weren't sure about selling the house?"

"No, things really did get busy, and I have a draft text that I thought I'd sent." He pulled out his phone and held it up for her to see. Busy. Let's meet up in person to talk. was in the text screen on his phone to her. "I didn't realize I hadn't hit Send until after you called me."

She didn't need him to prove that he'd meant to text her, but she appreciated the fact that he wanted her to know he hadn't completely ignored her. "Why don't you want to sell the house?"

"Oh, I want to sell the house," he said adamantly. "It's my brothers who are the problem."

"I thought you got their okay to sell?"

He glanced her way and half shrugged. "I brought up the idea to them in passing but that was about it."

Cierra cocked her head to the side. "That's not the same. Seriously, Wesley, you told me we were okay. I was ready to list the house later this week."

"I know."

Thankfully, she hadn't hit Send or told the other Realtors she knew that the house would be available. Instinct told her to wait until the house was officially up for sale. Thank goodness she'd listened to her instincts. "When were you going to get their okay? After we had a buyer ready to put down the earnest money?"

Wesley rubbed his temples. "No, I was going to tell them. I was hoping to show them how much the house is worth and how much we'd get for it. I was sure that once they knew that they'd be on board, but we went to the house over the weekend, and they flipped out over the changes I'd made."

She wasn't surprised to hear that. He'd flipped out when she'd first suggested making changes. Of course his brothers would also do the same.

Cierra shifted farther onto the couch to get more comfortable. "I'll be honest, I was surprised when you said you wanted to sell and even more so when you said your brothers were okay with selling."

He shook his head as if her words didn't make sense. "Why?"

"Because that house belonged to your parents. You and your brothers fought hard to stay together in that house after they died. I assumed all three of you wouldn't want to let it go."

"They don't," he grumbled.

"Do you?" When he gave her an *obviously* look, she shook her head. "Then tell me why."

He let out a heavy sigh. "No one is here. Dion's moved on. Tyrone's moved on. They both disappeared and left me here to take care of things like I always do. I don't want the responsibility. It makes more sense to just let the place go."

His brothers moving out of the house and away was a good reason to let the place go, but the second half of his statement was what gave her pause. "Do you not want the responsibility or are you more upset that they've gone and you're still here?"

He scoffed and shifted on the couch. His eyes skirted to hers and then away. "No, I don't need my brothers around to be happy."

She cocked a brow. "Be honest, Wesley. Because it sounds like you're about to start a fight with your brothers and possibly create a rift that can't be healed if you push this. So, tell the truth. What's the real reason?"

He sighed then leaned forward until his forearms rested on the tops of his quads. "I'm tired of being their fixer. The one who handles the stuff they don't want to handle. We all were supposed to take care of the house, but they just left it with me."

"Who took care of the place before your brothers moved away?" She knew the three of them lived there through high school, but once she'd moved away from Sunshine Beach and got married, she hadn't kept up with what was happening with Wesley and his brothers.

"Dion lived there."

"And how much did you and Tyrone do while he lived there?"

Wesley glanced away and rubbed his hands together. "We helped when he needed it. If there were any big maintenance costs, he'd let us know and we'd help out."

"But how often did he ask for help?" When Wesley only scowled instead of answering, she got her answer. She placed her hand on his knee. "I'm not saying it's your turn to move in there and handle things now that Dion is gone. That's something the three of you need to figure out, but what I will say is before you get rid of the house that means so much to you and your brothers, you should talk to them about how you feel."

"I don't want to sound ungrateful," he admitted.

"Ungrateful how?"

"The show is the reason they're all moving forward. I wanted the show just as much as Tyrone, but I didn't expect our lives to change so much. I wasn't ready to be left behind."

He spoke the words quietly and in a rush. As if he

didn't want to admit that was the real problem. His confession surprised her. He'd spent so much time in high school trying to be someone outside of his brothers' shadow. She would have expected him to feel the same now, but just like she'd changed since they were teens, so had Wesley. Not wanting to be in your brothers' shadow didn't necessarily mean being happy to be split from them or see them handle a big change in their lives and move on easily when he struggled.

She slid closer and rubbed his back. "Then tell them that instead of just putting the house on the market. Knowing your brothers, they would never leave you behind. They're your family and they love you. Trust them to understand how you're feeling. Then, maybe, the three of you can decide if selling the house is really the right thing to do or not."

He was silent for a few seconds before the corner of his lips lifted in a rueful smile. "Why are you always so good at getting to the point?"

She lifted a shoulder. "As someone who never takes no for an answer, I find it's easier to cut to the chase instead of beating around the bush. It's served me well so far."

He let out a soft chuckle. "That part of you hasn't changed since high school."

She patted his back. "Back then you were always so sure of yourself. It's why I liked you so much."

Wesley sat up straight and frowned at her. "Did you really?"

The sudden seriousness in his voice surprised her. "Really what?"

"Like me?"

She would have rolled her eyes if he wasn't watching her so closely. Had he really not known how much she'd been into him? She already knew the answer to that. He'd only said yes because she'd asked him to prom, not because he'd liked her or wanted to go with her. Hearing those words back then had crushed her heart. She could gloss over it and not dwell on the past, but she knew she wouldn't be able to fully trust anything they started now if she didn't address what happened then. That rejection had completely changed the trajectory of her life.

She met his gaze and spoke honestly. "I did. A lot."

"Then why did you break my heart before prom?" His words came out like a hot accusation.

Cierra snatched her hand back as if seared. "*Your* heart?"

He sat up straight. "Yes, my heart. You kind of flirted with me in chemistry lab and then asked me to take you to prom. I thought you liked me, but instead you dump me and go with my best friend Troy instead."

She lifted a hand. That was not what happened at

all. "Hold up. The only reason I changed my mind is because I overheard what you told Troy and the rest of your friends."

His brows drew together. "What are you talking about?"

She crossed her arms over her chest. "A week before prom, right before the pep rally, I heard you, Troy and all your little friends talking about me. You said you didn't really like me and only said yes because I asked. Of course I changed my mind after hearing that."

He continued to scowl. "I didn't say…" His voice trailed off before his eyes widened and he rubbed a hand over his mouth. A heartbeat later he cringed. "Damn! I remember that."

"Yeah, exactly. You were so happy to tell them you didn't like me. They all heard along with two of my friends on the cheerleading squad. There was no way I was going with you after that."

The pain and humiliation of hearing him tell a laughing group of friends that he didn't really like her had not only broken her heart, but it also shattered her confidence. Before then, she'd believed that she was good at reading people. That she could trust her instincts. Wesley's declaration made her believe she couldn't trust not only herself but how she viewed the way other people saw her. When Troy told her straight up the next day that he liked her and wanted to date her, she'd clung to his honesty after being fooled by her feelings for Wesley.

"Why didn't you say something to me?" The disbelief in his voice made her wonder if he believed it was easy to go up to the guy you thought liked you to demand an answer. Sure, maybe, if she hadn't first heard him declare to a room full of people that she wasn't his type.

"I was not going to chase after you. Why did you say that if you didn't mean it?" she tossed back at him.

"Because I was young and dumb and embarrassed about Troy teasing me in front of our friends for trying to get together with someone like you. Back then I wasn't used to admitting to what I wanted. When he kept pressing, I denied. I didn't think you'd hear it."

"That doesn't make it right. I was really into you, Wesley. That hurt. It's why I went out with Troy instead."

He took her hands in his. "I'm sorry. I know it's years late, but I hope you can forgive the teenage me for being a dumbass." The honesty and regret in his eyes and his voice broke through any lingering animosity. They'd been so young and impressionable.

"What about now?" she asked hesitantly. She wanted to believe they weren't as impressionable now that they were older, but she wouldn't make assumptions. "If someone presses you about liking me, are you going to back away again? Because I'm having a hard time not falling for you again, especially after you kissed me, and I'm not ready to be made a fool of as an adult."

Wesley squeezed her hands and stared into her eyes. "I'm not a teenage boy anymore, Cierra."

The confidence and resolve in his voice combined with the bold look in his eyes sent shivers over her body. No, he was not a teenager anymore. He was all adult and the realization hit her that this Wesley would not be easily intimidated.

He looked at her the same way he had at her house a few days before. A look that said he wanted to give her that third kiss he'd teased about and leave no doubt that he was interested. Heat flared across her skin. Her nipples tightened as need pooled between her legs. She wanted to kiss him, but she was in her office. She didn't have appointments, but a client could drop by. That reasoning was drowned out by the temptation of knowing no one was there to interrupt if he kissed her. Desire flared bright and hot in his eyes.

She swallowed hard. She had to break the spell before she did something impulsive and indecent in her office. "Oh, you're a man now?" She tried to sound teasing, but her voice came out a little breathless. Her hands were still in his. She tried to tug her hands away, but he didn't let go.

Wesley leaned closer to her on the couch. His voice low and his eyes dark hypnotic pools that put her in a sensual trance. "Very much so. And this man wants you."

Chapter Fifteen

Cierra tried to act like a lady. To act like she wasn't itching to jump on Wesley immediately. They were in her office after all. This was a professional space. Not a space for hopping onto a man, even if she was ridiculously attracted to him and wanted nothing more than to have his lips on hers.

What she should do is thank him, remember that she had to pick up Aria from school in less than two hours and schedule an appropriate time for them to go on an official date. Hopefully a date they'd end with more kissing and a healthy side of touching all the sensitive spots currently aching for his caress.

That's what she needed to do. Except what she needed to do and what she wanted to do often fought against each other. Years of trying to be a good wife and mother had programmed her to do the thing she should do. The right thing. The responsible thing.

She was tired of being good.

She leaned forward and traced her finger across his chest. "You want me...how?" Something flared in his eyes that made her pulse jump.

"Honestly?" he asked.

She nodded slowly. A slow heat built in her midsection and spread upward to her breasts and down toward the ache growing between her thighs. "Honestly."

He leaned forward and whispered in her ear. "I want you right here on this couch."

She sucked in a breath. She hadn't expected him to say that. To be so brazen and stare at her with such heat she was surprised her clothes weren't set on fire.

"Was that too much?" His lips brushed her ear.

She felt the tickle of his mouth against her skin across every inch of her body. Her stomach and sex clenched as she sucked in a breath.

She shook her head. His words were not too much. In fact, she wanted to hear more. Wanted to feel and experience more.

Wesley kissed the outer shell of her ear. "Should I stop, go home, and wait for a more appropriate time and place?"

The good, responsible person she'd tried to be for years would say yes. She was still technically at work. Her door wasn't locked. Anyone could come by the office and see her. See them.

Except she didn't have any appointments. No one just dropped in on her at work. All of her appointments and prospecting for new clients or agents were done for the day. The chances of anyone catching them were slim, but the idea of being caught, of the riskiness of it all, made her pulse pound in her ears. She hadn't done anything daring or remotely sexy in so long she knew she would regret sending him away for the rest of her life.

She turned her head and kissed his cheek. "This is the perfect time and place."

Wesley's eyes met hers. They scanned her face for a second before his lips covered hers. His mouth was soft against hers despite the passion behind his kiss. His tongue slid past her lips in a bold exploration that made her fingers dig into his shoulders. Wesley eased her back onto the cushions of the couch.

Cierra gasped and broke the kiss. "You really do want me right here."

His lips trailed across her cheek and jaw until they came to her ear. He gently nipped the sensitive lobe. "More than you'll ever know." His voice was deep and gravelly. Her body heated another hundred degrees.

Cierra pulled him closer. "Show me."

"Oh, I'm about to," he said with a naughty grin.

His body blanketed hers. Their kiss went from fast and fiery to slow and sensual. The heat and strength of him overwhelmed her. He kissed her with the same focus and commitment that he put into everything he did. His lips and tongue explored her mouth with tender, thorough strokes.

She arched her back until the tips of her breasts pressed into his firm chest. Wesley gripped her hips and she shifted, opening her legs so he could settle more firmly between them. The hard length of him pushed wonderfully against her aching core and Cierra groaned.

Wesley rotated his hips. Rubbing against her. "You like that?"

"Yes. Now stop playing with me," she said between clenched teeth.

She didn't care about the cocky light in his eyes. She needed and wanted this. His fingers slowly unbuttoned the front of her dress shirt, spreading it open until the black satin cups of her bra were revealed. He massaged one soft mound before pulling the cup down to expose her hardened nipple.

The trace of his tongue on her skin lit her on fire, but it was nothing compared to the explosion of pleasure when his lips finally wrapped around the aching tip. Cierra gasped and dug her nails into his shoulders.

"Why are you still wearing a shirt?" She jerked on the edge of his shirt until her hands finally spread across the hard, hot planes of his back.

Wesley leaned up enough to toss his shirt over his head. "Gone now."

"Good!" She removed her blouse and bra.

He kissed her again and the soft scratch of the hairs of his chest against her breasts made her wiggle against him for more of the sensual sensation. Wesley pushed up the hem of her skirt and then his fingers were tugging down the edges of her panties before brushing across the wet hairs covering her sex. He sucked air between his teeth before running his hand across her core again. "Damn, you're so wet."

Cierra didn't have a comeback for that. She just wanted him to keep doing what he was doing. Her head fell back, and her legs spread open. His fingers slid across and over her swollen clit in a thorough exploration that had her gripping his arms and lifting her hips for more. When he pushed two fingers deep, Cierra bit her lip to hold back the cry, but when he slid back and pushed in again, she let go of any pretense of holding back.

"Yes, like that. More of that," she practically moaned.

He repeated the movement, but she wanted even more. She jerked on the fastening of his belt. She wanted him naked, and she wanted him naked now. Wesley, sensing her urgency, made quick work of the buckle and the button. Then the sweet, thick length of him was pressed in all its hard glory against her swollen folds.

"Do you have a condom?" she panted out.

He nodded. "My wallet."

"Get it," she said between clenched teeth.

Wesley leaned back onto his knees and pulled his

wallet from his back pocket. She bit her lower lip as she watched him cover his length and had to stop herself from drooling at the idea of having him inside of her. His body was back on hers in a matter of moments and then he was filling her, stretching her, taking her to the heavens with one fulfilling stroke.

Their pace was steady. Their hips moved in synchrony. Wesley's mouth fell open and he squeezed his eyes tight. Cierra gripped the back of his head and pulled him down for another deep kiss. Their movements became frantic, less in sync, their breathing more ragged as the pleasure rose. She was so close, so, so close to going over the edge that she could taste it. Then Wesley twisted his hips in a way that pressed his body against her clit in just the right way to make her eyes roll to the back of her head, and her body shattered into a million delectable pieces.

Wesley couldn't focus on anything other than the way Cierra's lips moved as she ate grapes and talked while standing next to him in the small kitchenette in her office. After they'd caught their breath, cleaned up and got dressed she'd asked if he wanted a snack or something to drink. He'd been unwilling and unable to walk away from her after what they'd done and quickly agreed.

He'd expected things to be awkward or uncomfortable. They were anything but. Their ability to talk and be relaxed in each other's presence hadn't evaporated. If anything, he felt closer to her. He wanted to be closer to her. He wanted to keep her in his life.

That revelation scattered his thoughts even more. So much so that he almost missed it when Cierra said, "I know Sally Rutherford."

He blinked, jerked his eyes away from her tempting lips and met her gaze. "You what?"

She shrugged and picked another green grape out of the bowl on the counter. "I mean…I knew her. She's the grandmother of a friend of mine."

Wesley pressed a hand against the counter and leaned forward. "Wait, are you saying you know this woman?"

Cierra rolled her eyes and chuckled. "Were you listening to a word that I said?"

"Kinda," he admitted.

She shook her head. "I figured. Your eyes were trained on my mouth."

"Only because I want to do this." He brushed his mouth against hers. Cierra's lips lifted into a sexy smile that made him linger a few seconds longer than he'd meant to. This was why he couldn't leave. She was damn addictive.

He pulled back before he got distracted and took her back over to the couch. He lifted a hand. "Hold up. Before I forget what we were talking about. Tell me about Sally Rutherford."

Cierra pouted before grinning and leaning a hip against the counter. "I have a college friend named Alicia Rutherford. Turns out she lived in this area, but since I was at Sunnyside High and she was in Riverview High we didn't know each other. Anyway, we kept up after we both migrated back home after graduation. Her grandmother was named Sally. I only met her a few times, and she died about four or five years ago. I remember Alicia saying she was taking some of her grandmother's old things to the county museum. When I asked why, she just said it was what her grandmother wanted. I didn't think any more of it."

Excitement bubbled up inside him, and he grabbed her hands. "Do you know that you're amazing?"

She laughed and shrugged. "I mean…I kind of had a suspicion."

He pulled her into his arms for a tight hug. "You've just saved us a lot of time trying to track down the right person."

She pulled back and waved a finger at him. "Hold on. I mean, there could be another Sally Rutherford with ties to the DeWalt Manor. Alicia never mentioned her family having anything to do with the manor or the family."

"They have some type of connection," he said.

"If the Sally who donated is your friend's late grand-mother, then she had a bunch of the old records and files related to the DeWalt Manor. Are you sure your friend never said anything?"

Cierra nodded. "Very sure. If I would have known she had any connection to or knowledge of the place, then I would have asked her for help figuring out what was happening there before coming to you."

He frowned. "You didn't want to come to me?"

She cocked her head to the side. "Sir, why would I want to reach out to the guy who broke my heart in high school? Besides, you avoided all my calls and texts. I had to track you down. I guess you didn't want to talk to me, either."

He'd avoided her calls for the same reason she'd hesitated to reach out to him. He'd been a fool for being embarrassed about liking her back then. He frowned and slid closer to her. He placed a hand on her hip and stared into her eyes. "I shouldn't have avoided you. I guess I held on to that old embar-rassment just as much as you."

She wrapped her arms around his waist. "As long as I don't have to go through that again. I'm not going to catch you telling people that you slept with me on the couch because I asked you to, am I?"

Even though her eyes and voice were teasing, Wesley didn't laugh. "No. You won't. I meant what I said. Anything dealing with us is between us."

Her eyes went soft, and her body pressed closer to his. She bit the corner of her lip, and he was helpless to resist. He lowered his head and kissed her again.

The door to her office opened. "What the hell is this?" a male voice said.

Cierra and Wesley jerked apart and spun toward the door. His surprise quickly turned into irritation when he met Troy's gaze. What the hell was right. Did Troy just pop up whenever he wanted to?

"Troy?" Cierra said, sounding just as irritated as Wesley felt. "What are you doing here?"

"I needed to talk to you," Troy said as if it were obvious and Cierra should have anticipated his arrival.

"About what? I told you to call me before coming over. You can't just pop up over here like this." Cierra crossed the room and pointed toward the door.

Troy pointed at Wesley. "What's he doing here?"

"None of your business," Cierra said. She pulled on the sleeve of Troy's shirt. "Go."

"Wait," Troy said, planting his feet. "It's about Aria."

Cierra dropped her hand from his shirt and crossed her arms. "What about her?"

"It's my weekend with her." Troy glanced at Wesley. Wesley just stared back with what he hoped was a blasé expression. Even though he wanted nothing more than to kick Troy out, he was trying to respect that he was Cierra's ex and Aria's father.

"I know it's your weekend with her. And? Are you trying to say you can't watch her again?"

Troy looked back at Cierra and shook his head. "Nah, nothing like that. It's my grandmother's birthday. I wanted to make sure you were cool with me taking her to North Carolina for that."

Cierra placed her hands on her hips and grunted. "Seriously, Troy? You know I don't mind if you take her to see your grandmother. You could have called with that."

"I'm just saying. I wanted to be sure." He glanced at Wesley again. "If I hadn't shown up, would you tell me about this?"

She grabbed his arm and shoved him toward the door. "Once again, this ain't your business. Get out, Troy. Don't come back over here unless you call first."

He tried to argue but Cierra shoved him out of the door and locked it after he was gone. Wesley crossed the room to her. She had her back to him with her hand to her forehead.

"I'm sorry," she said in a quiet voice.

"For what?"

When she faced him, her gaze was wary. "Troy, popping in like that. He got better, but I guess he feels the need to start up again."

"Why would he start up again?" Was Troy bothering her? The idea made him want to follow Troy out and convince him, by any means necessary, to respect Cierra's wishes.

"Because he's got some stupid idea in his head that one day I'll change my mind and help him, in his words, 'get his family back together again.'" She rolled her eyes.

"He wants you back?" Wesley held his breath while he searched her face, the smallest amount of fear entering his chest.

"No," she said with enough ferocity to chase away his fear. "He just doesn't like losing. I'm the one who ended things. I couldn't take the lies and manipulation anymore. When I took charge of my life, he tried to hold on tighter. Troy's got his own life, a new woman and a real estate firm I helped build to what it is today, but he thinks he can still have a say in what I do. It's why I want to sell the DeWalt Manor and make my brokerage successful. We worked together at Huger Realty. I was one of the top agents and had the best sales. Better than Troy, but he wasn't good with that. He took out all our savings, borrowed money from anyone he could and bought out the firm without saying a word to me. Suddenly, he owned it, and then he held me back. Focused more on the other Realtors and tried to persuade me to give up selling houses completely and support him. That's when I left. I'll never go back."

"He did all that?"

She nodded. "Yep, and that was my last straw."

An unsettling thought hit him. "Do you think Troy worked things so you'd overhear what I said that day in high school? He knew I liked you, that's why he teased me so hard, but he didn't hesitate to ask you out after you broke things off with me."

Cierra scowled at the door then threw up her hands. "You know what, I don't want to think about that." When he opened his mouth to continue, she shook her head and wrapped her arms around his waist. "Seriously, if I dwell on the way Troy manipulated me in the past, then I'll never move forward. I'm done with him. We can't change the past, but I can learn from it. I can't control the future, either, but I can focus on what's in front of me right now. What I want at this moment and what brings me joy right now. That's what's most important. What about you?"

Wesley most definitely wanted to confront Troy. He wanted to know if the guy who was supposed to have been his friend had intentionally betrayed him. But when he looked into Cierra's eyes, he saw her resolution to focus on the here and now. Her determination to build a new life for herself, to be free of Troy and his influence and only commit to things that made her happy. He let go of the thoughts that stirred up frustration in his chest. He pulled her tighter into his embrace and savored the feel of her soft body against his.

"I'm all about focusing on us and what we have right now, Cierra."

Chapter Sixteen

Cierra reached out to Alicia Rutherford later that night and confirmed what she'd told Wesley. She hadn't remembered wrong, and Alicia's late grandmother Sally had donated a bunch of items related to the DeWalt Manor to the county museum. After Cierra mentioned she was trying to sell the manor for the family, Alicia immediately suggested they meet.

"Girl, there is some shady stuff going on at that place," Alicia had said, sounding as if she couldn't wait to tell everything she knew. "Stuff the family tried to hide. My grandmother used to talk about it all the time. Come over this weekend and I'll get my mom and my grandma's sister, Aunt Virginia, to come over, too. We'll tell you all we know."

Cierra didn't have to be told twice. That Saturday, Wesley picked her up and the two of them went to visit Alicia and her family. Alicia lived in a modest one-story home on a cul-de-sac in the older Cottontown neighborhood. Wesley parked in the driveway behind two other cars. Alicia greeted them at the door. She was the same age as Cierra, but shorter, with natural red hair, chestnut-brown skin and a bright smile.

She quickly ushered them inside and introduced them to her mother and great-aunt, who both looked like older versions of Alicia except her aunt's natural hair was completely silver. They shared the same complexion and welcoming expression and were short and curvy like Alicia. Cierra watched as the women fawned over Wesley and congratulated him on the new television show. Wesley may have said he was uncomfortable with the extra attention that came with doing the show, but he didn't show it. He was gracious and kind as he accepted the compliments and hugs offered by Alicia's mom and aunt. Still, she noticed the relief in his eyes when they finally stopped and motioned for Cierra and Wesley to sit down around the kitchen table.

"I really appreciate you taking the time to talk to us today," Cierra said once everyone was settled.

Alicia shook her head. "This isn't a problem at all. As soon as you said you were working with the family to sell that place, I knew you needed to talk to my mom and aunt."

Alicia's mom, Mary, nodded. "She's right. A lot of people don't know the history behind that place."

Wesley rested his arms on the table and watched intently. "The family has done nothing but talk about their spotless legacy."

Alicia's great-aunt, Virginia, grunted and pursed

her lips. "Their legacy is a pack of lies. Lies they put together to try and make the place look good while they made money."

Cierra leaned in. "What do you mean?"

"That family's been brushing the truth about the things that happened at that place under the rug for years."

"How do you know their secrets?" Cierra asked.

Virginia and Mary exchanged looks before Virginia spoke. "My sister worked for them. And our mom before that. They were housekeepers, you see. They always knew there was something fishy at that place. It being haunted wasn't a secret, but the way the family acted like they had no clue why it was haunted never sat right with us. Then one day, my sister found a bunch of items in the basement and started going through it. That's when she found out about the murder."

Cierra sucked in a breath. Her skin prickled and the memory of hearing the word *murder* come from that weird spirit box Wesley used came back to her mind. "What murder?"

"It was in a journal. An old one. Back when my sister worked there… Who's the girl who owns it now? Carolyn?" When Cierra nodded, Virginia kept talking. "My sister worked there when Carolyn's grandmother Patty was still alive. Patty kept a journal ever since she was little, and she wrote down what really happened there."

Wesley shifted in his seat. "What happened?"

"Her mother killed a woman in that kitchen," she said in a matter-of-fact voice. "The DeWalt family always tried to clean up their history. We know all the stories they tell about how good they treated the people enslaved there—so well many of them didn't even want to leave after they were free." She rolled her eyes with that part. "Everyone knows they were nothing but lies. But it didn't end with that. Well, in Patty's diary, she wrote about how her mother killed their family cook in the kitchen. She was a good cook. So good that Patty's mother bragged to anyone who would listen about having the best cook in the county. Well, when her cook's son was falsely accused of murdering the girl Patty's uncle was dating, the cook pleaded for the family to speak up on behalf of her son. Apparently, the girl and Patty's uncle used to fight a lot. The family refused and the cook was so upset she messed up a meal that was supposed to be for some important people. Patty's mother didn't like that and confronted her in the kitchen. An argument broke out and she got so mad when the cook said she quit, Patty's mother grabbed a knife and stabbed her in the back as she tried to walk out."

Cierra placed a hand over her mouth. "What?"

Virginia aunt nodded. "That's what Patty wrote in her diary that night. She saw the entire thing. She was about ten or eleven at the time. Of course, the family had enough money to cover everything up. Patty's father and some of his friends dumped the body in the wetlands near the river and cleaned everything up. Only the family saw, and they spread the rumor that the cook up and quit saying she was leaving town because she was so upset about her son committing murder. Soon after that the spirits started terrorizing the family."

"What happened to the journal? Did your sister have that?" Wesley asked eagerly.

Virginia shook her head. "No, Patty kept it and burned it from what I understand. After she went through the boxes, she told my sister she could have whatever else she wanted. Then she fired her the next day."

Cierra wondered if Patty regretted telling the story and that's why she fired Sally. "Why didn't your sister tell anyone this story?"

Mary shrugged. "My mom told people, but who was gonna listen to a Black woman spreading rumors about the DeWalt family? The cook's only family was her son, and he was tried, convicted and executed in no time. Patty didn't even remember the cook's name, or that's what she said. In the journal Patty just called her Ms. P. Sally wished we could know more, but other than that journal that's all we've got."

Wesley shook his head. "That's not all we've got." When they frowned, determination hardened his face. "We've got the spirit of the cook who was murdered. Maybe we can get something from her. Plus, we'll take this story back to Carolyn and see if she's heard it."

Alicia looked at Cierra. "Will this help you sell the house?"

Cierra doubted it. If the story were true, that gruesome history would make things harder. "I don't know who'll want a house where someone was murdered in the kitchen."

Wesley placed a hand over hers. "If this is the spirit, we can help her find peace. If we can do that, then maybe she'll move on and leave. If we do that, then you'll have an easier time selling the house."

Cierra nodded and took a heavy breath. She hoped that would work. Not because she wanted to sell the house, but because after hearing this story, she wanted nothing more than to resolve a murder that went unnoticed for far too long.

Wesley took Cierra back to his place after meeting with Alicia and her family. He'd asked if she wanted to go home, but she'd said she wanted to see where he lived. His condo wasn't much to check out. A modest two-bedroom place not too far from the Waccamaw River. His unit was located close enough to the pool that he could hear people laughing and splashing whenever he opened the back windows.

He poured them both glasses of wine and grabbed

two of the prepackaged meat and cheese snacks he typically kept on hand for a quick snack between meals and they settled on the shaded back patio.

"This is a nice place," Cierra said, sipping her wine.

"Thank you. I've lived here for about five years. I bought it as investment property, but it suits me and I haven't come up with a good reason to move."

"You never thought of moving into your family home once Dion left? You could make some money by renting this place."

He leaned back in the chair and studied the wine in his glass. "Not really. I don't want to take care of a house right now. I like my setup. I pay my fees to the organization, and they maintain the grounds, pick up the trash and take care of the pool. That's good enough for me."

Cierra chuckled. "You really aren't the home improvement type."

He shook his head. "I know enough to fix small things, but I'm no expert. Right now, I don't want all that comes with owning a single-family home."

"Is that part of the reason you want to sell?"

"Part of it. Now that Dion has moved, and Tyrone has never mentioned any plan to live there, it's more than I want to deal with on top of starting the show."

"You know you have to talk to them and come up with a plan. You can't sell the house without their agreement."

Wesley sighed and sat up. He placed slices of cheese and salami on a cracker while he considered her words. "I know. Believe me, I heard you loud and clear the other day. I'm going to talk to them. I'm just not ready to talk to them right now."

His brothers continued to text and tell him he was wrong for trying to sell. Them not listening to his reasons and focusing only on him "doing whatever he wanted" proved they always expected him to roll over and accommodate them. He had to figure out a way to make them listen.

Cierra nodded and took a long sip of her wine. "Okay, but don't put this off too long. Pretend it is for me if that'll make you call them sooner."

"Do you need the commission from selling my place?" She was working hard to grow her business and mentioned needing to make money.

She shrugged. "I do, but not at the expense of coming between you and your brothers. Honestly, the DeWalt Manor will do more for me than selling your house. Since we know what's going on, is there anything we can do?"

"Now that we have an idea of who the spirit is, I can do a little more digging. If I can confirm the story, maybe we can do something to help her move on and find closure. Once that happens, you should find it easier to sell the house."

He'd like to say he couldn't believe the story Virginia shared, but he'd researched enough spirits to never rule anything out. People killed for all sorts of reasons. Feelings of disrespect or loss of power were typically at the top of the list.

"How do you do this? I mean, deal with the stories and remain calm?"

"Not all stories are as bad as what we heard today."

"But a lot of them are?"

Some were worse, but she already seemed upset by what they'd learned, and he didn't want to upset her further. "If I can do something to make people feel better and safer in their homes, then that's a win. That's why I do what I do."

"I appreciate you helping me with the manor. I was nervous when my dad gave me the recommendation. I didn't think I'd be able to sell the place. You've given me hope."

"Do you mind if I ask a question?"

She raised a brow. "I won't know until you ask."

He chuckled. "Fair enough. What made you open your own realty firm? Was it because of what Troy did?"

"That's part of it. I was good at selling houses. My clients liked me and I was one of the top sellers. Plus, I was good at mentoring and encouraging the new agents. I mentioned to Troy that I wanted to open my own brokerage. He always had a reason why I shouldn't. We didn't have the money. Dealing with agents wasn't worth the effort. It was easier for us to work for a name like Huger Realty than try and be competition. I believed him and suppressed my dreams. When he bought the business without telling me and then made a point of giving all the best houses to other agents and pushed me further to the back because he wanted me to focus solely on being his vision of a good wife and mother, that's when I knew he would never support or encourage me in doing anything else."

Some of the best things about Cierra were her drive and confidence. He couldn't imagine trying to dim her light. "Did he really expect you to stay?"

She sighed and settled back in her chair. When she spoke again, regret filled her tone. "Why wouldn't he? For most of our relationship I listened to whatever Troy suggested. I did everything I could to be supportive of him, and realized too late that Troy wouldn't support any dream I had. He always came up with a reason why I couldn't do something, but he always said it in a way that made it seem as if he were looking out for me."

"He was like that as a friend, too. I remember back in high school he'd pretend to be on my side, but later I realized he was just trying to keep me from doing what I really wanted. It was the same with liking you. He knew how much I liked you, and how embarrassed I was for people to know. That's why he teased me about you in front of our friends."

Her chest puffed up and her eyes narrowed. "You

never explained why you were embarrassed for people to know."

Embarrassment blazed his cheeks, but he wouldn't deny how insecure he'd been back then. "Because you were out of my league."

"Say what?"

"I'm serious. You were vibrant, popular and every guy in the school wanted you. I was cool because of my brothers. I didn't think I had a chance with you."

She stared at him, speechless for several seconds before blurting out, "I can't believe you couldn't tell I liked you."

"A lot of girls were nice to me, but that didn't mean much. In middle school I had a crush on another girl. When I asked her to be my girlfriend, she said she just saw me as a friend. After that, of course I didn't believe you were interested."

Cierra let out a wry laugh and shook her head. "And I thought you were too above it all to be interested in me."

"What does that mean?"

"You were so unbothered by everything in high school. You didn't do cliques. You weren't into any school gossip. You just minded your business with your books and blasé attitude. You seemed so mature and cool. I thought you thought I was too immature to date."

"Immature?" That was the last description to

come to mind when he'd thought of Cierra. "You were beautiful, confident and amazing. You were not immature."

"I mean, didn't you go out with a girl in college?"

Wesley shook his head. "It was a friend of my older cousin and we just went to the movies once. And she was a college freshman with a late birthday. She wasn't that much older. Troy spread the rumor about me dating older girls to try and make himself look cool by association."

"Doesn't matter. 'Wesley dated a college girl' was all I knew."

He reached over and took her hand. "I guess we both were mistaken."

"That made it easy for Troy to slip in and keep us apart." She sighed. "I meant what I said. I can't change the past, so I'm not going to feel bad about it. Who knows if we would be here now if we'd got together back when we were so young."

"That's true. Still doesn't make me less pissed about what Troy did."

"I get that, but he's not worth it." She leaned on the edge of her chair and placed a hand on his arm. "What's happening now is worth focusing on."

Her touch was soft and warm and immediately he thought about the way she'd grabbed and held on to him in her office when they made love. His body stirred. He leaned toward her and kissed her. He meant to make it brief, but the softness of her lips beckoned him to linger, taste more. So he did, deepening the kiss until her tongue brushed against his and his heart imitated a prize fighter beating the hell out of his ribs. When he finally pulled back, they were both breathless and he spoke softly against her lips. "What's happening now is good enough for me."

Chapter Seventeen

Wesley went back to the county museum later that week. Now that he had a better idea of what had happened at the DeWalt Manor, the records of transactions and other documents were even more important. He had a rough idea of when the cook may have been killed, but he wasn't sure if the old records at the museum would give him any clues.

Once he told Dave, the museum director, the story, he became so excited that he agreed to help go through the books in the box again. After two hours Dave looked up, eyes wide, and frantically tapped the ledger on the table in front of him.

"I think I found something."

Wesley's head popped up from where he scanned through another ledger. "What did you find?"

"The name of the cook. It looks like she signed off on deliveries for about six months. It suddenly stopped around September of nineteen forty-one."

"What's the name? If we have her name, then we can find out the name of her son, if it turns out she has one, and verify his story." Wesley slid his chair closer to Dave's so he could get a good look at the ledger.

Dave pointed to handwriting on the book. "Pearly Mae Tribble." Dave's eyes were wide and solemn. "Is that enough to go on?"

Wesley stared at the name written in neat, cursive handwriting. "I've worked with less."

Dave looked back down at the ledger. "Do you really think the story is true?"

"I've learned to never be surprised by anything. First thing is to see if I can find information about Pearly Mae. If she had a son and what happened to her son."

Dave cocked his head to the side. "That doesn't mean we can prove he was arrested wrongfully."

Wesley nodded. "We may not have physical proof, but if I talk to people who may remember what happened or see if someone revisited the case later, I may come up with another kind of proof."

Wesley stared at the name in the book. If the story were true, and the family had murdered Pearly Mae in cold blood and dumped her body, then he wanted to try to help her restless spirit find peace. Not only that, he felt a need to bring closure to this case.

Wesley called Cierra after leaving the museum and gave her an update. She was out showing a property with a new client and agreed to drop by his place when she was done. He needed to work on a fire station renovation for a small town in the area. Instead, he decided to see what he could find through an internet search on Pearly Mae Tribble and her son.

There wasn't much, but he found an article about a young man, Lou Earl Tribble, originally from Sunshine Beach, who was put to death in 1941 at the age of fifteen. The write-up about people wrongfully accused and later put to death was brief and mentioned Lou Earl having no family around after his mother ran off, after he was accused of the crime. The five sentences in that article were enough to make Wesley's blood turn cold. The story Alicia's grandmother heard may be true.

The doorbell rang and sucked Wesley out of his research. He closed his laptop and went to the door. Cierra looked professional and radiant in a fitted navy suit that accentuated her waist and drew his attention to her legs where the skirt stopped just above her knees. Her hair was loose, parted on one side and framed her face in soft waves. He immediately wanted to pull her into his arms and kiss her, but the scowl on her face made him pause.

"What's wrong?"

She shook her head. "It's nothing."

He stepped back to let her enter. She came inside, her shoulders stiff and her lips pressed into a thin line. Unease spread through his stomach. "No, it's not nothing. Tell me what's wrong."

She waved a hand. "It doesn't have to do with you." She went farther into the house. "Tell me what happened at the museum."

Wesley followed her into his living area. Before she could sit down, he came up behind her and placed his hands on her shoulders. The muscles were rigid beneath his fingertips. He gently massaged before leaning forward to kiss her cheek. "Talk to me."

She sighed and the tension in her body eased slightly. "Do you really want to hear about my drama with Troy?"

He didn't. In fact, he could go the rest of his life not hearing about Troy. But he cared about Cierra. He didn't like seeing her obviously upset and stressed out. Therefore, he swallowed his immediate *to hell with Troy* response and reminded himself that he was an adult, and he could behave like one.

"I'm here to listen and let you vent. I won't give advice unless you ask for it."

The muscles beneath his hands relaxed even more. With his hands still on her shoulders, he guided her toward the couch. He sat in the corner of the couch and pulled her down to sit between his legs with her back to his chest. He resumed his shoulder massage. "Talk."

She sighed. "It's an ongoing battle. He doesn't want to pay for after-school care even though he's supposed to. So, he doesn't and they call me for payment."

"Why doesn't he want to pay?"

"Because if I would have stayed with him, then Aria wouldn't need after-school care. He wanted me to be a stay-at-home mom. While I admire the women who are, it was never something I wanted."

"Doesn't he know you won't be coming back?"

"He does. I thought we were good the last time I went off on him, but now he's acting out."

Wesley bit his lip. Was he the reason Troy was lashing out? Troy's dislike of Wesley's relationship with Cierra was obvious. The last thing he wanted was to cause her more problems.

"What are you going to do?" Her shoulders had stiffened again and he increased the pressure until her body relaxed into his.

"I'd take over myself, but I need him to cover after-school. At least until I can get the DeWalt Manor sold. If I do that, then I really don't need him for anything. I can tell Troy to kiss my ass while I take care of Aria without any help from him."

"Until then, can you make him do what he's supposed to?"

"I could go back to the courts and get him for not following the terms of our divorce, but that's more of a fight than I want. I'll figure it out."

"You know if you need anything I'll help. Just say the word."

She stiffened and pulled away. "You don't have to pay for anything for me."

"I'm just saying. I want to help."

"And I'm just saying, I don't need your money." She slid farther from him on the couch.

Wesley held up his hands defensively. "I didn't say you want my money."

"I didn't bring this up for you to offer to be a knight in shining armor." They spoke at the same time.

Wesley waved a hand back and forth in front of his throat in a cut-it-out motion. "Hold up. Let's start this over. What's the real problem? Because this sounds like a lot more than you not wanting my help."

She pressed a hand to her temple and closed her eyes. "Sorry. It's just…I swore not to be dependent on another person after my divorce. I spent a decade being told to minimize myself and rely on someone else to make decisions. I was manipulated into feeling bad for wanting to be independent. It's hard to unbreak that."

He took her hand in his. "I'm not asking you to unbreak that today. I just need you to recognize that I'm Wesley. Not Troy."

"I know that."

He lightly squeezed her hand so she would meet his gaze. "No, for real. I need you to understand that and know that. I won't treat you like any of my exes. I hope you won't do that with me."

"You mean like the woman at the farmer's market," she said in a teasing voice.

"Yes. Like her. I know you're not her. I won't treat you like you're her."

Cierra blinked. "Why is she an ex?"

"We dated. Things didn't work out, but we're still cool."

Her eyes narrowed. "Cool like she calls you once a week and you go over there to change lightbulbs and stuff?"

He shook his head. "Cool like we're civil when we see each other, and I don't have a problem supporting her business when I need a certain infused sugar to make a cake. A cake I brought you, remember."

"I don't know if I like you using her sugar to make me a cake."

"And I don't know if I like you assuming my offer for help is a way to manipulate you like Troy did. I get it. We're new. But take me at face value unless I show you something different. Okay?"

She stared for several seconds then leaned forward and kissed him. "Why are you so cute when you're all serious?"

"Now you're trying to distract me."

She grinned and slid her hands over his shoulders. "Is it working?"

It was. He was ready to lay her back on the couch and forget the reason she was over there. "I didn't call you over for this."

"I know. You found out something at the museum. Something that can help."

"How did you know?"

"Because your voice was all excited when I called." She leaned closer to him. Her eyes sparkling with mischief. "I like it when you get excited."

"You were pissed off a second ago. What happened?"

"You happened. Being all honest and straightforward. I believe I like straightforward in a man. It's sexy."

Oh, he could be very straightforward. "You want to hear about what happened at the museum now or do you need to vent some more?"

"Why?"

"Because if you keep looking at me like that, I'm going to take you to my bedroom."

She bit her lower lip and glanced at her watch. "I've got to pick up Aria in a half an hour."

A half an hour wasn't nearly enough time for him to do everything he wanted, but it was just enough time for him to help distract her. He didn't know what to do about her problems with Troy. He wasn't even sure if he was in the right position to try to do something. What he did know was that as long as she was with him, he wouldn't let her leave with a frown on her face or worries creasing her brow.

Wesley shifted to his knees on the floor. He

gently spread her legs. "I can do a lot in a half an hour."

Cierra's eyes widened. "What are you doing?" She covered her mouth as if shocked, but it didn't hide her smile.

His hands slid up her outer thighs, beneath the hem of her skirt, to the waistband of her panties. "Giving you something else to think about."

"You are so bad," Cierra said as she lifted her lips.

Wesley grinned as he slid her underwear down her thighs. He shoved them into the pocket of his pants before pushing up her skirt and spreading her legs. "Since when is it bad to please my woman?"

Whatever she was going to say came out as a low moan as he leaned in and used his lips and tongue to give her ultimate pleasure.

Chapter Eighteen

"Are you messing around with Wesley Livingston?"

Cierra was about to take a sip of the cola she'd taken out of her parents' fridge while thinking about the way Wesley intimately kissed her before she'd left his place. The question from her mom in her don't-play-with-me voice surprised her so much she dropped the can.

The soda clattered against the linoleum floor and the dark liquid stretched into a puddle. "Sorry!" She crouched and picked up the now-dented can. She quickly carried it to the sink and placed it there before taking the entire roll of paper towels off the holder.

"I take that as a yes," her mom said in a dry tone. She watched Cierra frantically swipe at the spilled soda.

"What? Why?" Cierra tore off more paper towels and put them down to stop the slow spread of the spill.

"You wouldn't have dropped the soda and had guilt splattered all over your face."

"I don't have guilt on my face."

"Yes, you do. It's the same look you used to have when you were a kid. So, tell me, how long have you been fooling around with Wesley Livingston."

Cierra didn't look at her mom and continued to wipe up the spilled drink. Who in the world had said something? She didn't suspect Cetris. She and her sister had long agreed to never rat each other out to their mom, especially when it came to their love lives.

"Who told you that?" she asked instead of confirming or denying anything.

"Aria," her mother said smugly.

Cierra stopped midswipe and frowned up at her mother. "Aria?" There was no way Aria would use the words *fooling around*. Plus, besides the few times she'd been around Wesley, Cierra made sure to not mention him for fear of her daughter getting too attached too quickly.

Her mother nodded slowly. "Yes, ma'am."

Cierra rose and put the soaked paper towels into the trash can. "Tell me exactly what she said."

Her mom went to the pantry and pulled out the wet mop. "When I picked her up from after-school, she was telling me about what she did over the weekend at Troy's grandmother's. I was half listening as she talked about all the fun stuff they did at the party and then she mentioned that Troy also told his mom that you were fooling around with Wesley."

Cierra's jaw dropped. "What!"

"Yes, and that's not all. Aria went on to tell me that if you were messing around with Mr. Wesley she's okay with that because he makes good cake?" Olivia said the last part with a raised brow.

Cierra closed her eyes and groaned. "He does make good cake."

"Excuse me?" Her mom's voice was scandalized.

Cierra opened her eyes and took the wet mop from her mom. "Calm down. Wesley likes to bake. He brought over a coffee cake and cinnamon rolls."

Olivia put a hand to her chest. "Oh, he's bringing food over. Cierra, what's going on? Are you really dating that guy?"

For a split second she considered denying. The disbelief and hint of disappointment in her mom's voice sparked a small flare of guilt. A flare she immediately stamped out. She had nothing to feel guilty about. She was divorced. Over three years divorced. She hadn't dated anyone since her marriage ended and she wasn't exposing Aria to anything negative.

She stood with her legs wide. One hand on her hip and the other clutching the handle of the mop. "Yes, Mom, I am dating him. Is that a problem?"

Her mom blinked before crossing her arms. "I'm not saying it's a problem. I'm just saying you should be careful about what you're doing because Aria is watching."

"Aria isn't seeing anything she shouldn't. This is a conversation for Troy. The one who brought it up in front of her and talked about me and my private life with his mom with our daughter within earshot." She ran the mop over the floor with angry, jerky strokes.

"Troy is concerned."

"Troy was hoping I'd lose my mind and take him back like a fool. That's the only thing wrong with him."

"Well…why wouldn't he hope you two could work things out?"

Cierra stopped mopping the floor to stare at her mom with disbelief. "Mom, seriously. You're not still on this. I'm not going back to Troy. I'm never going back. I left him for a reason."

"He only wanted to build something great for you two."

"He only lied about spending all of our money. Made huge financial decisions without talking to me first. Kept things from me and tried to make it seem as if my questions were proof that I didn't trust him instead of admitting that my questions were always spot-on."

Her mom sighed and held up a hand. "Fine. I'm not going to argue with you about this."

"There is no argument. My marriage is over. We're working together to give Aria the best we can, but that's it. Love don't live there anymore."

"I said fine, Cierra." Her mom's voice firmed.

Cierra sighed and went back to cleaning the spot where the soda spilled. After a few seconds, her mom spoke again.

"Do you like Wesley?"

Cierra stopped and looked up. "I do. I wouldn't date him if I didn't."

"I mean…do you really like him?"

"What do you mean?"

Her mom shrugged. "Do you think this is serious or is he just…scratching an itch?"

Cierra rubbed a hand over her face. "Did you really say that?"

"I want to know. If you really like him, then invite him over for dinner and let the family meet him. If it's just for fun…well, I understand you may have needs and—"

"That's enough! Please, let's stop." She held up a hand. Olivia pressed her lips together, but thankfully didn't interrupt. "I do like him, but it's a little too early for the meet-the-family thing. He's helping me with the DeWalt Manor and until we get that figured out then I'll wait on the big where-is-this-going talk."

Her mom's eyes widened. The concern in her gaze now switching to a calculated look Cierra knew meant her mom had just come up with one of her "brilliant" ideas. "You know, this could be good for you."

SYNITHIA WILLIAMS   215

"In what way?"

"He just got that TV show with his brothers, right?" Cierra nodded and her mom continued. "Well, he's pretty much a celebrity. You being connected with a celebrity will help recruit new agents and clients. Especially if he helps you sell the De-Walt Manor. You two will be a powerhouse."

Cierra raised a brow. "Are you really suggesting I stay with Wesley because it'll help my business?"

"I'm just saying there are benefits. Remember those."

Cierra shook her head and finished cleaning the floor. "Okay, Mom." She wasn't about to draw out this conversation by entertaining her mom's suggestion. Her mother, bless her, may have given up her career as a lawyer, but that didn't mean she no longer tried to find the best angle and get a win out of any situation.

She finished cleaning the floor and moved the conversation to the latest with the Literacy Council's prom. Her mom's belief that Cierra being with Wesley would help her do better was enough to satisfy her mother's curiosity for now. If her mom was satisfied, then she wouldn't take Troy's side if he came to her with any nonsense about Cierra dating again. And she had no doubt that would happen, because Cierra was definitely going to remind Troy once again that her relationship with Wesley wasn't up for debate or discussion.

Chapter Nineteen

Wesley and Cierra met with Carolyn DeWalt later that week at a small café in downtown Sunshine Beach. The three sat at a table next to the window that overlooked a small courtyard garden. Sunlight filtered in through the window, creating a cheerful glow off the soft yellow and green decor inside. A bright contrast to the dark news Wesley had to share.

Wesley shifted in the uncomfortable white chair and pushed away the dainty teacup with small lemons and green leaves painted on the sides. There wasn't much on the menu that appealed to him, mostly fancy sandwiches and salads, but he managed to find something to order. This was technically Cierra's meeting with her client. He was here to back her up with what he'd learned.

Because it wasn't his meeting, he sat in the dainty chair, drank the cucumber-infused water and forced a grin through the small talk instead of jumping right into asking Carolyn for everything she knew about Pearly Mae Tribble and her son. Cierra was much better at small talk and easing into things. She'd always been good at making people feel comfortable and at ease. Today was no different.

After they ordered their food and the server walked away, Carolyn clasped her hands in front of her on the table and gave Cierra an eager look. "Have you found someone to purchase the manor?"

Cierra gave a slight shake of her head. The sleeveless black blouse she wore had a small cutout in the front that drew his eye to the tantalizing view of cleavage beneath, and the ivory pants she'd paired them with hugged her hips. "I haven't sought out buyers just yet. I thought you'd like to know what we found out about the haunting."

Carolyn's brows drew together. She darted a glance at Wesley before looking back to Cierra. "I know that has been a hindrance before, but I didn't think that would be all you focused on. I want to get rid of the house."

"I understand, but getting rid of the house also means you have to know what's going on there so that potential buyers I bring aren't scared off like before."

Carolyn glanced around the room. The other tables weren't close enough for anyone to hear them, but she still looked as if she didn't want anyone to know the manor was haunted. It wasn't as if that was exactly a secret.

"I don't know who or why that's happening at the house," Carolyn said. "It really is a mystery."

Wesley couldn't hold back anymore. "Did you ever hear about a journal kept by your grandmother?"

Carolyn's frown deepened. "A journal? I don't think so."

Wesley watched her for signs of deception, but she appeared genuinely confused. "What about Sally Rutherford? She used to work for your family. Did you hear of any rumors she may have spread?"

Carolyn pursed her lips for a second and shook her head slowly. "I mean, the name sounds familiar, but by the time I was old enough to pay attention to what was happening my parents had switched over to professional companies for cleaning, building upkeep and maintenance. No one from the family has lived in the manor for years."

"We went to the county museum and found ledgers that were given to Sally Rutherford by your grandmother. When your grandmother gave them to Sally, she also told her a story about a former cook named Pearly Mae Tribble who worked there."

Carolyn shifted in her seat and her shoulders tightened. "When I was younger, I do vaguely remember my grandmother having a housekeeper. But that was years ago. What story did she tell?" Carolyn didn't sound affronted or upset, simply curious.

Wesley looked at Cierra and she nodded. He updated Carolyn on what he'd found out. Starting with how Sally Rutherford found the information at her grandmother's home and ending with what they'd heard after talking to Ms. Rutherford's family. Wesley had searched the town records and found more information on the case. After Pearly Mae "disappeared" it took the jury ten minutes to convict her son. He was executed by the electric chair soon after. As they talked the blood slowly drained from Carolyn's face.

The server returned with their food. Carolyn sat back and stared off into space while the server placed their food on the table and asked if they needed anything. Carolyn gave an absent wave of her hand to the question. Wesley and Cierra exchanged a look.

Cierra spoke when the server walked away. "Does any of this sound familiar?"

Carolyn blinked and focused on Cierra. "This is the first time I've heard this story…but…" Her voice trailed off.

Wesley and Cierra exchanged a glance. He nodded for Cierra to prod after Carolyn continued to stare blankly at her food. "What is it, Carolyn?"

Carolyn blinked rapidly before glancing at Cierra. "My grandmother struggled with her memories later in life. Once she mentioned her uncle killed a girl and that a…a Black boy took the blame. I was so shocked I tried to ask for more but then the thought was gone and her memory had her telling another story. I asked my mom, and she said she didn't know anything about that, but the look in her eye made me wonder. I pressed, and all she said was that her great-uncle Ray had been a mean, terrible man and that if he did kill someone she wouldn't be surprised. That was the end of that. My grand-mother's health declined and I didn't think about the story anymore."

"You didn't want to find out the truth about some-one else getting blamed for a crime your mom's great-uncle could've committed?" Wesley said, try-ing not to sound accusing.

Carolyn met his eye and straightened her shoulders. "Honestly, no. I never knew. He died before I was born, and no one talked about him except to say he had a temper and was hard to get along with. All I had was the ramblings of an old woman and that's it. There wasn't much I could do then. What can I do now?"

Cierra placed a hand on his arm before turning to Carolyn. "We can verify if Pearly Mae is the spirit in the kitchen. We can try to bring their story to light and clear her son's name."

Carolyn's frown deepened and she took a deep breath. "Let me reach out to some distant rela-tives. They don't have any interest in the manor, but they're older than me and may have more of the story."

"Are you okay with Wesley and his brothers

going back to the manor?" Cierra asked. "They can find out more."

Wesley's shoulders stiffened. He didn't plan to call in his brothers. He wasn't ready to talk to them after they'd disagreed about what to do with the family house. He didn't know if Cierra's suggestion was because she wanted to quickly finish the investigation and get on with selling the house, or if this was a soft nudge for him to reconcile. Regardless, he begrudgingly admitted to himself that he wanted his brothers there. They were invested in this story, and they would want to see it through to the end.

Carolyn nodded. "Yes, feel free to access it and do what you need to do."

Cierra smiled and sat back. "Thank you. Don't worry, we'll find a way to make this work out for everyone."

The following weekend, Wesley, his brothers, Cierra and Carolyn met at the manor for the investigation. Wesley asked his brothers to come straight to the manor rather than his condo or the family home beforehand. He didn't want to potentially ruin the vibe by rehashing their argument from the weeks before. That was probably why they didn't say anything either about meeting up ahead of the investigation. Bringing negative energy with them could influence what they discovered.

Just before they were to go inside, Tyrone tapped

Wesley's shoulder and pointed to Cierra. "What's she doing here?"

Wesley glanced at Cierra talking to Carolyn before looking back at his brother. "Carolyn is her client."

"That doesn't mean she needs to be here to sell the place."

"She wants to know what happened as much as we do. That's all."

Tyrone raised a brow. "Are you sure?"

"Why else would she be here?"

Tyrone shrugged. "To make sure we don't mess up her money," he said in a judgmental tone.

"She's not here because of money. She cares."

Tyrone didn't look convinced, but he held up a hand. "Let's get started."

Wesley decided to table that discussion for later. The group went inside and prepared for the investigation. They went through their normal routine of explaining to Carolyn about their equipment, what they were going to do and what they hoped to find.

Dion took the lead as he often did when they worked together. "Let's start in the kitchen since that's where we believe everything started."

Everyone agreed and they made their way to that part of the house. The second they crossed the threshold, Wesley shivered. The welcoming feeling he'd sensed when first entering the house evaporated as he crossed the threshold into the kitchen.

The angry aura made his skin tighten and he sucked in a breath.

Dion glanced his way, concern in his eyes. "You okay?"

Wesley nodded. "I think she's here, and she's angry."

Tyrone placed a hand on his shoulder. "Let's see what we can find out."

Wesley gave his brother an appreciative nod. Despite the disagreement still lingering between them, he knew his brothers would always look out for him. An inkling of guilt for rushing to put the house on the market twisted in his stomach. Maybe if he'd spoken up and been honest about his feelings the way Cierra suggested, they could've avoided the entire blowup.

Cierra slid closer to his side, her body tense and her lips pressed together. Wesley rubbed her back. "Ready?"

She smiled up at him. She tried to look brave even though he saw the uncertainty in her eyes. He wanted to lean down and kiss her right then. If they were alone, and not investigating a potential eighty-year-old murder, he would. Instead, he squeezed her hip before turning his attention to Carolyn.

"We're going to see if we can get any answers. Let's find out if the spirit making things harder for your family is Pearly Mae."

Carolyn hugged herself and glanced around the

room nervously. "I asked an aunt if she knew a Pearly Mae who once worked for the family. She didn't want to admit anything, but after a while she said there were rumblings about something happening, but she never knew the full story. That it was best to leave things alone."

"Some secrets don't follow a person to the grave," Wesley said. "Sometimes they linger."

Carolyn rubbed her hands up and down her arms. "Apparently so."

Tyrone held the night vision camera while Wesley operated the spirit box to try to communicate. They introduced themselves, said they only wanted to help and get answers before asking a series of questions. It didn't take long to confirm the identity of the spirit as that of Pearly Mae. As they asked more questions about her, her wrongful death and her son, the animosity in the room decreased, until there was no longer rage and anger but a deep sadness.

They checked other areas of the house just to be sure and encountered three other spirits. When they asked questions, the only response they received were first names: Mary, Ginny and Saul. Whenever they repeated the names, Wesley felt a sense of gratitude as if happy their names wouldn't be forgotten.

Carolyn was visibly shaken by the time they finished and went back outside. Her face was nearly as pale as the white shirt she wore, and her lips were pressed into a tight line. The group gathered around Dion's SUV to put away the equipment they used.

"I never knew," Carolyn said in a tight voice.

Cierra let out a long breath. "Her death was covered up so easily. It's sad and scary."

Wesley agreed with her. Knowing the other spirits only wanted their names to be spoken led him to believe they belonged to some of the enslaved people who'd also lived and died at the house. "Most of the stories of the people who died here were suppressed or covered up. They only want to be heard. For people to know they're here." People who would be forgotten if Wesley and his brothers hadn't investigated the manor.

"Maybe that's why they made selling the manor so difficult," Cierra said. "Selling would mean what happened here would be further forgotten. Pearly Mae's story would never be told."

Dion sighed and ran a hand over his head. "As if she and her son were nothing."

Carolyn ran a hand through her hair. "I've got a lot to think about." She looked at Wesley. "Thank you for this. You didn't have to help open my eyes to the truth of my family's history, but I appreciate you taking the time and inviting me here."

"It's important for you to know as well."

She nodded tightly. "I'm going to go home, pour a stiff drink and think about everything I heard here tonight."

"I'll give you a call tomorrow or the next day," Cierra said.

"Okay. Thanks again, Cierra."

They watched as Carolyn got into her car and drove away. Cierra turned back to Wesley and his brothers. "I guess I'll head off, too. I'm sure the three of you have *a lot* to talk about." She glanced pointedly from him to his brothers then back.

Wesley didn't need an interpreter to know what she was implying. She wanted him and his brothers to work things out about the family home. Even though selling the place would benefit her in the long run, she wouldn't push the sell if it meant coming between him and his brothers. Wesley loved that about her. Her willingness to put what was right above profit. If he were honest, he loved a lot more than that about her.

Tyrone grunted. "You mean about selling our family home so you can get the commission."

His brother's accusation startled Wesley like a slap to the face. He pushed Tyrone's shoulder. "Man, stop that."

Tyrone held up his hands. "What? Isn't that the truth?"

Cierra's lips lifted in a tight smile. "The commission off this place is going to do a lot more for me than selling your family home. Why don't you focus on the real reason why your brother is so willing to sell instead of taking your anger out on me?"

Tyrone's eyes narrowed in on Wesley. "Real reason?"

Wesley moved closer to Cierra and placed a hand on her shoulder. "I'll deal with my brothers."

"Please do," she said with a twist of her lip.

Wesley couldn't help but smile. She wasn't a pushover. He loved that about her, too. "I'll give you a call later, okay?"

She met his eyes and the frustration his brother brought up disappeared. Her lips lifted in a sexy half smile and she nodded. "Okay."

Not caring that his brothers were watching, he leaned down and brushed his lips across hers. "Be careful on the way home."

"I will." She gave Tyrone one last eye roll before nodding at Dion and then meeting Wesley's eyes. "Good night."

After she got in her car, he turned to meet his brothers' wary gazes. "Okay, let's get this over with."

Chapter Twenty

The brothers went back to their family home to talk. Dion and Tyrone didn't say anything when they entered. Their eyes just narrowed, and their shoulders tightened as they looked over the interior with many of the old furnishings removed. That was enough for Wesley to know their feelings.

They didn't immediately dive in. After such an intense investigation, they all needed a moment to process their feelings and the energy left from the house. They went to their separate rooms, showered and changed into basketball shorts and T-shirts. An hour later they reconvened around the kitchen table.

The kitchen, rather than the living room or family room, was the best place for their talk. The kitchen was the room with the least number of changes. There was no need to further rub salt in their wounds by making them sit in one of the re-decorated spaces.

Tyrone put a bottle of gold rum in the middle of the table along with a two-liter of cola. Dion opened a package of red plastic cups and filled them with ice. In silence, each of them mixed a rum and cola to their preferred strength, took a sip and sighed.

Dion spoke first. "So what's the real reason why you want to sell the house?"

"Isn't it obvious?" Tyrone said. "Cierra got in his head and now he's ready to get rid of Mom and Dad's house."

Wesley closed his eyes and sought patience. "This has nothing to do with Cierra getting in my head."

"I still think it was her idea," Tyrone said, sipping his drink.

"Redecorating the house so it can sell faster was her idea, *after* I brought up my interest in selling the house. I had the idea after talking to Calvin. Long before I ever brought it up to Cierra."

Dion's brows drew together. "Calvin? Calvin Kennerly? How did he give you the idea?"

"Because his parents' house sold as soon as they put it on the market. Because he told me about the sell when I was here cutting the grass and trying to work that damn Weed Eater. The same weekend you two were supposed to be here helping me but weren't."

"Cutting the grass and a conversation with him made you want to sell the house?" Tyrone sounded confused.

"Cutting the grass alone. Realizing that you two have both moved on. Being left behind to handle all of this." Wesley waved around the kitchen indicating the rest of the house. "Without either of you asking if I wanted the responsibility or even helping me come up with a plan for how we're going to handle the house."

"It wasn't like that," Dion said.

"Oh yes it was," Wesley cut him off. "You handed me the keys and said 'take care of the house' right after you packed up your stuff and left to surprise Vanessa. Right after that we went into the negotiations around and the filming of the show, and you—" he pointed to Tyrone "—took every opportunity to leave. You talked about moving to Atlanta or somewhere else. You both had reasons for why you couldn't help me do anything with the house. It was just assumed that Wesley would handle everything."

Dion shrugged but didn't quite meet Wesley's eyes. "I didn't think you'd have a problem with it. You're here. I figured—"

"No, you assumed I would just sit back and take care of things. That I would step in and keep things smooth and easy for you while you two moved on with your lives. You didn't think about me, what I wanted or anything else. Just like…"

Dion's eyes snapped to his. "Just like what?"

If he was going to do this, he might as well go all the way. "Just like after Mom and Dad died."

"Hold up," Tyrone said, shifting anxiously in his seat. "What are you talking about? We all stuck by each other after that."

"Yes, we eventually did. But let's be real, right after Dion stepped up it was hard. You spiraled, Tyrone. You and Dion were always fighting. I had to play peacemaker. I stepped up to keep you both happy so you wouldn't argue and we wouldn't get split up. I wouldn't change that, but it's tiring being the cushion for you two and not once getting any kind of appreciation."

"We appreciate you, Wes," Dion said. "You know we do."

"Nah, I don't. I'm happy about the show. Really, I am, but a part of me wishes things were like they were before. At least then I had my brothers around when times were hard. Now I'm here. Alone. And you two just walked away without a backward glance."

They were silent for several seconds before Tyrone spoke. "Wes, no matter what happens I'll never just walk away from you. I mean, yeah, the show was my dream and now it's come true. I'm loving everything about this ride. I'm not going to lie. It's like for the first time in years I feel free to just… live. I never planned to leave you or Dion behind, I just needed some space."

Dion nodded. "I guess I felt a little of the same. Meeting Vanessa and leaving a job I'd had since I was nineteen was scary as hell but also exciting. I didn't have—" He cut off abruptly.

"The weight of responsibility that came with raising us," Wesley finished.

"Yeah, I guess that's what it is. But still, I didn't view it as leaving you behind. It was just me doing what you both always told me to do. Live for myself."

"I know. You both are doing what you've wanted and what you deserve. For me it felt like I was being forgotten."

"I never realized how much you did to keep us together," Tyrone said, staring into his cup. "Not until just now. It's true, you did help keep me and Dion from killing each other back then."

Wesley thought back on all the fights he'd broken up between them and shook his head. "It was *The Dion and Tyrone Show* all the time. I was just a side character."

"Nah, you were never a side character," Dion said. "You were the voice of reason. You were the glue. You still are. I guess that's why I didn't think twice about leaving the responsibility for the house to you. You always just handled stuff. I didn't realize you didn't want to handle this."

"It's not that I don't want to handle it. In fact, the more I look at the place the more I think about us living here. It's hard to imagine someone else here."

Tyrone nodded. "No matter what happens, this is home. I don't want it to go."

Dion shook his head. "Neither do I, but if you really don't want to take care of it, then maybe we should consider selling."

"I don't want to sell. Not really," Wesley said

and realized he meant it. He hadn't known how to be honest about his feelings with his brothers before. Now that he had, he didn't want to lose the one thing they had. The center and heart of their family.

"Then how about we come up with a plan to take care of the place. We'll figure out yardwork, house care and the bills. Maybe we'll even consider renting the place. Something that works for all of us," Dion said.

Tyrone nodded. "I'm cool with that."

Wesley nodded. "So am I."

Chapter Twenty-One

Carolyn called Cierra the next day. Cierra sat at her desk wrapping up the finishing touches on the details of a property she planned to list the next day, as Aria sat on the floor next to her coloring. Her heart stuttered in her chest when she saw Carolyn's number. She hadn't expected to hear from her so soon and planned to give her a few days to process what she'd learned and Cierra time to come up with a fantastic idea of how to handle the property.

Less than twenty-four hours was not enough time to come up with a fantastic idea. At this point, Cierra had no idea what to do about the manor. Selling the house would benefit her business immensely, but she didn't feel right capitalizing on the property knowing the history.

Cierra answered the phone. "Hey, Carolyn."

"Hi, Cierra, did I catch you at a good time?" Carolyn's voice sounded high-pitched and hesitant. Cierra wondered if she wanted this to be a bad time so she'd have a reason to end the call without getting to the point.

"Yes, it's a good time. I'm wrapping up my day before taking my daughter to the craft store. What's up?"

"Oh, okay, good. Well, I want to talk to you about the manor."

"Yeah, I've been thinking about yesterday and what we learned. I've been trying to think of good options."

"Oh really? What did you come up with?"

Nothing. "Well, I haven't had the chance to talk to Wesley yet. He may have some ideas of what can be done."

"You don't want to get rid of the ghosts, do you?"

Cierra couldn't tell if that was hesitancy or excitement in Carolyn's voice. She shook her head even though Carolyn couldn't see her. "No. Never that. I just hoped I could find a way to ease their heartache and pain."

"I know. It's all I've thought about since last night. Honestly, I don't feel right selling the place. Not to someone who'll turn it into another wedding venue or bed-and-breakfast. Or worse, someone who'll tear down the house and divide the land into a bunch of small parcels and turn it into a subdivision."

"I feel the same," Cierra said. "It would just be another step toward burying the history of what happened."

"I don't want to bury the history anymore," Carolyn said, sounding solemn.

An idea crossed Cierra's mind. One that would preserve the history of the place but may not do much for her bottom line. In fact, it wouldn't do anything for her bottom line. She tried to call up the business-minded side of her brain. The side that told her to put emotions aside and just worry about getting out of the red, helping her fledgling firm succeed, finally proving to everyone that she could succeed without the help of Troy. Tried and failed.

"You know, you could donate the manor to the historical society," Cierra said before she talked herself out of it.

Carolyn was quiet for several moments before speaking. "Do they take donations?"

"I'm not sure how the process works, but I could reach out to them. Talk to them about the history and see if they'd like to turn the manor into a museum or cultural center. Not only would that preserve the home and the land, but we could also tell the truth about what happened to Pearly Mae."

Carolyn responded immediately, excitement clear in her voice. "That isn't a bad idea. Do you think they'll go for it?"

Cierra waited for the regret to turn up. The enthusiasm from Carolyn meant the chances of taking back this idea were slim to none. The regret didn't appear. Damn her and her good heart. At this rate she'd never get out of the red.

"I'll call them tomorrow and set something up."

"That would be great. Thank you so much, Cierra. When your dad mentioned you were great at this, he was right. You've helped me figure out a difficult situation."

"It's no problem at all. I want to preserve the history and tell the truth about Pearly Mae."

They spoke for a few more minutes before hanging up. Aria stopped coloring and stood. She came over and laid her head on Cierra's shoulder. "Did you sell another house, Mommy?"

Cierra let out a humorless laugh and patted her daughter's head. "Not quite."

"Then why are you smiling? I thought you needed to sell more."

"I do, baby, but sometimes it feels just as good to do the right thing."

Cierra took Aria to the craft store after getting off the phone with Carolyn. The trip was a good way to shake off the disappointment of knowing she wasn't going to get the sale she needed. She didn't regret her idea to approach the historical society, but she also couldn't deny the sting of knowing she might not be able to keep the doors of her struggling real estate brokerage open.

She'd wanted to prove to Troy and her parents that she could make a living on her own. More important, she'd wanted to prove to herself that she could do it. She'd gone from her parents' house, to college, to marriage with Troy. The past three years were the first years she'd lived independently and completely supported herself. Despite the struggle, she'd enjoyed making her way and proving she could start a business and raise her daughter. Now she had to face facts. She would have to get another job to help bridge the gap. Keeping her firm open while working for someone else would be next to impossible. So, honestly, getting another job meant letting go of her dream.

Aria tugged on Cierra's hand. "Mommy, can I?"

Carolyn blinked and focused on her daughter. She'd been so lost in her thoughts that even though her brain registered Aria's happy chatter, she hadn't really listened to what she said.

"I'm sorry, baby. Can you what?"

Aria, thankfully, didn't appear upset by her mom's unfocused attention. She just grinned up and pointed at the shelf. "Can I get the paint set, Mommy? Please?"

Cierra looked away from her daughter's expectant eyes toward the display case. Sure enough, several paint kits were on the shelf. Outlines of puppies, kittens and farmhouses with the paint and brushes included. Cierra's brows drew together. So far, Aria had only explored her creativity with markers and colored pencils. She wasn't sure about setting her daughter loose with paint.

"I don't know if it's washable," Cierra said.

Aria tugged on her hands again and pouted. "I promise to be careful. Please, Mommy, please. Daddy let me paint when I went to Grandma's house. I didn't hardly mess up anything."

"Hardly mess up anything" meant something had been messed up. Cierra had some old sheets she could put down. Or they could paint outside on the patio instead of in the house. She was just about to agree when a male voice chimed in.

"Of course you can have the paint kit. Daddy will get it."

The sound of Troy's voice made Cierra's shoulders tighten. Her gaze jerked away from the paint kits to the end of the aisle where Troy stood. Behind him stood a brown-skinned woman with short, stylish hair and a red button-up shirt that barely fastened over her ample breasts and tight black pants.

Cierra suppressed her sigh when her eyes met Tia's. The girlfriend Troy tried to pretend didn't exist whenever he begged Cierra to come back but most people in town, including Aria, knew he had. She didn't have anything against Tia. Cierra was pretty sure she and Troy had got together after the divorce. If anything, she felt sorry for the woman. Clinging to a man as manipulative as Troy.

"Daddy!" Aria said in a delighted voice before running toward Troy. He knelt and gave her a big hug. "What are you doing here?"

Troy straightened and pointed to a large picture

frame in Tia's hand. "Tia needed to buy that, so we stopped in. I didn't expect to see you both here."

"Mommy came to buy me new art supplies. But she's worried the paint will mess things up. Tell her I didn't mess up too much."

Troy looked at Cierra. "Of course you didn't mess up too much. Your mom is just overly cautious. You know she worries about things more than I do."

Cierra took a fortifying breath to stop herself from snapping at Troy. "I was just about to say yes."

Troy came close and picked up a kit. "Don't worry about it. I'll buy the kit and you can paint it at my house, what do you think about that?"

"Thanks, Daddy!" Aria said, grinning.

Cierra's eyes narrowed. He'd got the kit with the farmhouse. Aria had pointed to the one with the kittens. Cierra picked up that one. "No need. I've got it. Why don't you save that money for the after-school payment?"

The smug smile fell off Troy's face. She hated to be petty with him, especially in front of Aria, but she also wasn't about to stand for the "good parent/bad parent" routine he tried to play. Cierra tried not to badmouth Troy in front of Aria, but doubted he offered the same courtesy. Her mother finding out about her and Wesley was proof enough of that.

"Well, we wouldn't need after-school if—"

"If what, Troy? We were still married?" She gave an exaggerated look over his shoulder at Tia. "I think we both can agree that we're better off separate. Am I right?"

Troy looked back at Tia. Her chin has risen, and her lips were pressed into a thin line. If he wanted to go there, then she would.

After a few tense seconds, Troy's face broke into a no-worries smile and he held up a hand. "We're both happy now. What's most important is taking care of Aria."

Cierra nodded. "Agreed. Have a good night, Troy. Aria, say goodbye to Daddy."

Aria nodded and waved at Troy. "Goodbye, Daddy."

Cierra took her other hand. She gave a stiff nod to Tia, who sniffed and glanced away before walking out of the aisle and toward the front of the store. Cierra sighed and shook her head. If Tia wanted Troy, she could have him.

Troy and Tia ended up standing a few people behind her and Aria in line. Their whispered argument carried just enough for Cierra to tell they were arguing about her, but not loud enough for her to hear everything. She tried to ignore them as the other customers in line focused on the two.

"Don't compare me to Cierra because we are not the same," Tia said in a raised voice.

Everyone in line went silent and eyes swung toward Cierra. Heat filled Cierra's cheeks. She didn't know everyone in the craft store, but one of her mother's fellow Literacy Council members was in line behind Troy, and the young girl at the register sang in the choir at her parents' church, and she could swear the woman right behind her she'd met at Cetris's job.

Thankfully, she was next and was able to check out. She quickly paid for the paint kit and ushered Aria out of the store. Troy and his girlfriend were coming out just as Cierra backed out of her parking spot. She didn't bother to give them a second glance, even though Aria waved as they drove by.

"Mommy, do you think Daddy is going to marry Ms. Tia?"

The question was so unexpected Cierra almost slammed on the brakes to turn to her daughter. Instead, she adjusted the rearview mirror to meet Aria's gaze. "Have they talked about getting married?"

"She brings it up, and Daddy always says 'we'll see.'"

"Do you want him to marry her?"

Aria pursed her lips and pulled the kitten paint kit out of the bag next to her. "I don't know."

"You know Mommy and Daddy aren't going to get back together, right?" she asked carefully.

Aria nodded. "I know. I was thinking, if Daddy married Ms. Tia and you married Mr. Wesley, then that might not be so bad."

"Who said anything about me getting married?"

"Grandma did. She said you and Mr. Wesley

make a good power couple. I asked what that means, and she said you'll make a lot of money. I want you to make a lot of money so you don't have to worry about selling houses so much. Plus, he's nice and makes good cakes. So, maybe it'll be good if you marry him, and Daddy marries her."

"Um…well, it's too soon to talk about marrying anyone. But understand you'll be the first to know if I do decide to get married. Okay?"

Aria met her eyes in the rearview mirror and smiled. "Okay."

Cierra smiled back then readjusted the mirror. Her hands gripped the wheel as frustration, annoyance and something else swirled in her midsection. She couldn't believe her mom was already planning her marriage to Wesley. And saying something about it in front of Aria! She and Wesley had just started dating. The last thing their new relationship needed was for her mom to start the town's rumor mill going about her and Wesley getting married. She wasn't even sure if she wanted to get married again. She hoped that word didn't get back to Wesley before she had time to clear the air.

Chapter Twenty-Two

Wesley studied the two office chairs on display in the office supply store. He'd narrowed down his selection to the two, and just had to decide which one to purchase. His chair at home was on its last legs, and after he'd got up with a sore back after spending the morning working on a design for a client, he finally accepted that the best decision was to replace it. Instead of buying one online and hoping the reviews were accurate, he'd opted to come into town and select one personally.

"What are you thinking? Do you want to sit in them again?" the clerk, Nathan, asked.

He'd patiently helped Wesley go through the options of chairs and went over the pros and cons while he'd narrowed down his choice.

Wesley took a deep breath and pointed to the chair on the left. "I'm going to go with the one that's more ergonomically suitable. I spend a lot of time at my desk. I need the support."

Nathan nodded. "Excellent choice. I'll get one from the back. Do you need us to assemble it for you?"

Wesley waved a hand. "No need. I can put it together."

"Sounds good. I'll meet you up front at the register. Just give me a few minutes to pull the chair from the back."

"Thanks, I appreciate your help."

"No problem at all."

Wesley took one last look at the display chairs and smiled. Now that he'd finally made the decision, he grinned and rubbed his hands together. He must be getting old if the thought of a new office chair made him this excited. He stopped himself from taking a picture and sending it to his brothers. They'd just clown him for being geeked out over office furniture. He'd wait and take a picture when he'd assembled it at home.

He'd also send the picture to Cierra. Maybe see if she'd like to come over and see the chair herself. That would be a very transparent way of trying to get her to come to his place, but he didn't care. He wanted to know how she was doing after the investigation. He'd spent the weekend with his brothers coming up with a plan for the house and hadn't had the chance to check in on her. And tell her he wasn't selling the family home anymore.

He also missed the hell out of her but didn't want to be too clingy. They'd just started dating. He wasn't sure what she expected of the relationship. Wesley wasn't into quick flings or trying to see a bunch of different people. Porcha had been his last serious relationship. After they broke up he hadn't been in a rush to start something new, but he was still interested in settling down. Cierra was recently divorced and ready to build her own life without the help of her ex-husband or anyone else. Did that mean she wanted to get into another serious relationship, or did she just view him as a quick fling?

He pushed aside his uncertainty about his relationship with Cierra and walked to the front of the store to wait for Nathan with his chair. As he hovered near the registers the sliding doors opened, and three older Black women walked in, laughing and chatting. Wesley prepared to nod and step aside when his eyes met those of Cierra's mother.

Her smile widened and she waved. "Wesley, is that you?"

Wesley held up a hand and nodded. "Yes, ma'am, it's me."

Olivia came over with her other two friends. "Well, speak of the devil. I bet your ears were burning."

Wesley tugged on his right ear. "Not really. Should they be?"

She lightly slapped his shoulder before taking his wrist in her hand and pulling him closer to her two friends. "Ladies, you know Wesley, don't you? Him and his brothers just got the new television show where they're investigating ghosts."

The women both nodded. Wesley pasted a polite smile on his face and nodded. The women were vaguely familiar but growing up in a small town meant he was vaguely familiar with a lot of people. He wouldn't say he knew them.

"I know your brother Dion," one of the women said. "He fixed the pothole in my road a few years back. Such a sweet boy."

Wesley nodded. "Yes, ma'am, that's him." He didn't know what else to say to that. It wasn't unusual for someone to meet him and mention how they knew Dion or Tyrone instead of him.

"How is he doing?" she asked.

"He's good. In Charlotte now. He'll be getting married soon."

The woman's eyes twinkled, and she patted his arm. "He's not the only one, I hear."

He pursed his lips. He didn't know of anyone else getting married. He was out of the town's gossip circles. For all he knew someone in the woman's family was getting married. "Oh really?"

Cierra's mom pressed a hand to her chest. "Oh, Sandra, don't tease him. You'll embarrass him."

Wesley looked between the three women. "I'm not following."

Olivia winked at him as if he were in on some secret. "I was just telling the ladies about you and

Cierra dating. I'll admit I was initially worried. I mean, with her starting anew after the *divorce*." She lowered her voice on the word as if it were a bad thing. "But honestly the two of you together is a good thing. You're definitely going to be the town's next power couple."

Wesley blinked. "Power couple?" They'd just become a couple. He wasn't aware of any power that came with that.

Sandra spoke up. "Olivia was just telling us about how you were going to help Cierra's new company."

"Not directly," Olivia said. "But you see the obvious benefit of them being together. Now that she's dating a television star and selling the DeWalt Manor, she's going to be remarkably successful. Like I said, the new power couple."

Wesley stared at the women and took in their expectant faces. Not sure what to do, he blurted out the first thing on his mind. "We didn't get together to be a power couple."

"Of course you didn't," Olivia said but smiled as if she and Wesley were in on some big secret. "It just worked out that way."

Nathan came up with the boxed chair Wesley was purchasing in his arms. "Sir, are you ready?"

Wesley nodded. "Yeah, thanks." He looked at the women. "That's mine. It was nice seeing you."

"Nice seeing you, too. You two are coming to the prom together, right? It'll be good for you both to be seen together at the event. With your new show and all. We're excited to spotlight you both."

Wesley stood stunned. He and Cierra hadn't talked about the prom. Unsure what else to do, Wesley nodded slowly. The women waved and went on into the store. Wesley followed Nathan to the register. He absently went through the motions of paying for the chair and making small talk with the cashier. He refused Nathan's offer to carry the chair out to his car and did it himself.

The entire time his brain buzzed with the awkward conversation he'd had with Cierra's mom. Here he'd been worried he was being presumptuous wondering if he and Cierra would turn serious when her mom was telling her friends, and who knew who else, that he and Cierra were the new "it" couple. Not to mention the hint of a future marriage.

Cierra hadn't mentioned telling her parents about them. He'd thought they were keeping things between them until she was ready to introduce him to Aria as her boyfriend. What had changed? Did she want them to be the new "it" couple? Did she view being with him as an advantage to her business? He didn't want to believe that, but her mom had pretty much insinuated as much.

A weird feeling spread through his midsection. He didn't want to believe Cierra would do that, but after all these years she hadn't contacted him until she'd needed help with the manor. Right after he'd got the television deal.

Wesley got in the car and drove out of the parking lot. He didn't like his train of thought. Before he let suspicions get the best of him, he would go to the source. He'd talk to Cierra before he jumped to conclusions.

Wesley arrived at Cierra's office right before she would have closed. In his rush to find answers he'd forgotten to call to make sure it was okay if he dropped by. He hoped he wasn't interrupting her with a client. If so, he'd apologize and hurry away. He was probably overreacting, but he wanted to get to the bottom of this before his imagination had a chance to push him from mildly concerned all the way to paranoid.

The open sign was prominently displayed in the window. He went in and the chime above the door announced his arrival. Cierra sat behind her desk and looked up. Her dark brown eyes widened and her lips lifted in a bright smile.

"Wesley? What are you doing here?" she asked, sounding surprised more than upset about him popping in.

She looked great in a sleeveless red button-up shirt that enhanced the glow of her smooth brown skin. Her hair hung loose around her face and dangling gold earrings sparkled in her ears. He immediately wanted to cross the room, pull her into his arms and kiss her. So much so that he took several steps in her direction, his feet and instincts guiding him to do that before his brain caught up with the movements of his body.

Aria's head popped up from behind the desk and Wesley froze midstep. She grinned at him before running around the desk. "Mr. Wesley! Did you bring more cakes?"

Wesley's gaze dropped to Aria, who stopped in front of him, her hands clasped together and a huge expectant look on her face. She was so adorable that Wesley couldn't help but return her smile.

"Not today. I came by to talk to your mom about something else."

Aria's eager expression didn't go away. "Is it about getting married? I told Momma that I hoped you two would get married."

"Aria!" Cierra said and stood quickly.

Wesley blinked and focused on keeping the smile on his face from turning into a scowl. Maybe his suspicions were warranted. Why else would Aria also bring up the idea of marriage? Was Cierra so open with her plan to turn them into a power couple that even Aria knew?

Cierra rushed around the desk and put her hands on Aria's shoulders. "Don't say that?"

"Why not? I told you I'm okay with it."

"But it's not something to talk about right now,"

Cierra said. "Why don't you go into the other office and get your new paint set. We'll take it over to Grandma's house."

Aria nodded. "Okay. Be right back." She waved at Wesley then went through a door at the back of the office.

When the door closed, she turned back to Wesley. "Sorry about that. Aria's got it in her head that…" Cierra waved a hand. "Never mind. I'll talk to her about that later. I'm sure that's not why you came by."

That was what he'd come by for. Cierra wanting to quickly brush aside the conversation didn't raise his confidence. The embarrassment in her eyes made him want to believe he was rushing to conclusions. That all of this was some type of misunderstanding.

"Was it about your house?" she asked before he could answer. "Did you convince your brothers to sell?"

"Nah, we've decided to keep the house," he said.

"Oh." She stepped back. Her brows drew together. "So they didn't agree with you."

"We came to an agreement about taking care of the house. None of us wanted to sell it. Even you knew that. Why do you look like something's wrong?"

She shook her head and smiled but it wasn't as bright as before. "Nothing's wrong. I just…I don't know, thought maybe I'd still have that sell."

Wesley frowned. "Is that what this was about? Selling my house?"

"What are you talking about?" she asked, sounding confused.

"The reason why you're with me. To sell the house?"

She crossed her arms under her breasts and eyed him warily. "Where is this coming from?"

"From seeing your mom at the store earlier and her saying we're the new 'it' couple. That us being together will help you grow your business and that's one of the reasons we're together."

Cierra's hands dropped and her mouth fell open. "What? My mom didn't say that."

"Yes, she did. In front of her friends. We haven't even talked about marriage but already your mom and Aria are talking as if this were a given."

Cierra held up a hand. "Hold up. Is that why you came over here? To ask if I'm only dating you to get something out of it?"

"I don't want to believe it. That's why I felt it was better to talk about it."

"You should already know the answer."

"It shouldn't be a big deal for me to ask what's up after what your mom said."

"Yeah, if you realized that my mom is spouting nonsense, but not because you actually believed I'd use you like that."

"You seemed disappointed when I said I wasn't selling the house."

Her eyes darted away. "I wasn't disappointed."

"Yes, you were. First you were telling me to sell, then not to sell, and now you're wishing I were selling. I mean, what's up, Cierra? Are you really interested in me or what you can get from me?"

Her jaw dropped. She scoffed and shook her head. "You know what? Get out." She pushed him toward the door.

"What?"

"You heard me. Get out. I spent a decade with a guy who wasn't there for me and I'm not about to sit around and take crap from another one. Until you can come at me with some sense, don't come here at all."

"But—"

"No buts." She opened the door and shoved him out. "Bye, Wesley." The door slammed in his face before he could say another word.

Chapter Twenty-Three

Cierra and Aria arrived at her parents' home an hour after she kicked Wesley out of her office. Aria ran toward her grandparents as soon as they entered the house. She'd called Cetris to tell her what Wesley had said, and per usual, her sister talked her down before she proceeded.

"You know Mom can do the most. She probably freaked him out. I don't blame him for asking."

"But he should know I wouldn't do that."

"Yeah, but you still can't get mad that he asked. And try not to go all angry-daughter on Mom. You know how she is. She's probably just happy you're dating again after you left Troy."

"I can't let this slide."

"I didn't tell you to. I'm telling you to talk to her rationally and not just because you're mad at Wesley. Mom listens when we're calm. You know that."

"Can you come play referee?" she'd asked with a slight whine she wasn't afraid to use on her sister.

Cetris had laughed her off. "No, ma'am. I told Lil Bit I'd meet up with her for mani pedis," Cetris had said, referring to one of her friends. "Plus, I don't need Mom prodding into my love life. Call me after and let me know how things go."

Which is why Cierra didn't say anything immediately when her parents were all smiles and hugs as Aria showed them her paint set. Cierra even held off while they set up a plastic tablecloth on the back patio for Aria to paint. Once they had Aria set up at the table with her paint set, Cierra and her parents sat nearby in wicker chairs and watched Aria have fun with her art.

"So how are things going with the DeWalt Manor?" her dad asked. "Are you getting closer to putting the place on the market?"

"Not quite." Cierra glanced over at Aria happily painting and oblivious to them.

"Why not? I know you've sold a few houses here and there, but the reason I tried to connect you with Carolyn was because I know you need this sell. Are you going to be able to keep your firm going without this sale?"

She wasn't sure. Without that sale and now the loss of Wesley's house, her plans of recruiting new agents and keeping her business open were nearly lost. She understood Wesley's reasons not to sell. But she had felt a second of disappointment when he'd confirmed her suspicions. She was happy him and his brothers came to a compromise despite how it affected her bottom line.

"We found out what's happening at the manor, and after discovering the truth, Carolyn doesn't feel comfortable selling it."

Her mom frowned. "Doesn't feel comfortable? What does that mean?"

Cierra updated her parents on the results of the investigation and what she and Wesley had discovered. "After we confirmed everything, Carolyn was shaken. Honestly, so was I. That's why I suggested donating the house to the historical society. They can preserve the place and tell the stories of everyone who lived and worked there."

Her dad shook his head and grunted. "I remember my parents talking about Pearly Mae. They never believed she would just abandon her son like that."

"You know the story?" Cierra asked, surprised.

Her dad's lips twisted into a sad smile. "A lot of people suspected she didn't really run off, but there was no proof."

"Carolyn no longer wants to hide the truth about what her family did."

Her dad nodded. "Well, I can understand why you both came to that decision. I admire you for trying to do the right thing, and I believe the historical foundation would be happy to get ahold of the manor."

"But?" Cierra asked, seeing the worry in her dad's eyes.

He sighed and met her eyes. "But, I'm concerned

about you and that realty firm you're trying to keep going. There are a lot of other Realtors in the area with bigger names behind them and the resources to advertise. I supported you when you opened your business even though I didn't agree with your decisions. Now that you won't have the DeWalt Manor to sell, what are you going to do?"

"I'm not giving up, if that's what you're thinking," she said in a tight voice. "I'll find a way."

Her mom leaned forward. "Have you talked to Wesley about being a celebrity spokesperson for your firm? Maybe you can offer his services whenever you buy or sell a house. That would be good publicity."

Cierra scoffed and stared at her mom. "I can't just offer up Wesley like that."

"Don't say it like that. I don't mean in a bad way. You two are dating. If he wants you to be successful, wouldn't he be willing to help you out?"

"We just started dating. I'm not with him because of the television show. So can you please stop telling your friends we're getting married and embarrassing him?"

Olivia's head jerked back. "I didn't embarrass him."

"Yes, you did. He came to my place questioning why you're hinting around about us being the next power couple and possibly getting married."

Her mom sniffed and lifted her chin. "What's wrong with wanting what's best for my daughter?

What have we always told you? If you're going to do something, do it to the best of your ability and get the most out of the situation. Whether you like it or not, you dating a local celebrity will benefit you and there's no need to pretend otherwise."

"That doesn't mean we have to make it the main focus on our relationship. Wesley is not enjoying the extra attention he's getting from the show. He's having a hard time with the shift from being a regular citizen to someone people want a piece of. Can't you see how my mom coming up to him talking about us being a power couple and taking over the world could make it look as if I'm not dating him because I like him?"

Her mom pursed her lips and sat back. Cierra raised her brows and waited. She looked at her dad and he gave her an I'm-not-in-this shrug. Out of respect, she didn't roll her eyes. She knew he felt the same way as her mom, but her dad stayed out of things whenever she and her mom debated.

"Mom?" Cierra asked carefully.

Her mom sighed. "Fine. You're right. I won't do that anymore." Her brows drew together. "Was he really upset?"

"He was. He accused me of just dating him for what I can get out of it."

"Did you two break up? I hope you didn't break up because of what I said." Concern entered Olivia's voice.

"Don't worry about it. We're adults. We can figure this out. Without parental interference," she said with a pointed look.

Her mom nodded. "I'll stay out of it, but that doesn't mean I'm going to pretend like I'm not happy to see you two together."

"Why, because your daughter is dating a celebrity?"

Her mom shook her head. "No, because my daughter is finally happy and seeing someone. You know how I felt when you left Troy—"

"Very much so," Cierra said dryly.

Her mom gave her the evil eye and Cierra shut up. "You know how I felt when you left Troy. I hoped you two would work things out. When you didn't and you focused on the business, I worried you'd never slow down and find something or someone to make you happy."

"My job makes me happy."

"Your job is your way to prove to all of us that you can make it on your own. You think we don't know that? You want it to succeed, but that's not the same as being happy. I want you to be happy, Cierra. That's all we've ever wanted."

Her dad nodded and gave her a your-mom-is-right smile. Despite her earlier frustration, warmth spread through Cierra's chest. She knew her parents wanted the best for her. They told her that constantly. Even when she disagreed with their methods, she understood they pushed her because they wanted her to succeed. That didn't lessen the joy and love in her heart after hearing them say it.

Aria jumped up from the table and ran over with her wet canvas. "Momma, look. I finished the kitten."

Cierra sat forward and gingerly took the canvas into her hands to take a look. Aria had painted the kitten a dark orange color. "It's beautiful, baby."

"Thank you. Now I'll do the rest." She kissed Cierra's cheek before taking the canvas to show her grandparents.

Cierra smiled as she watched them ooh and aah over Aria's painting. Her mind went to Wesley, and she wondered how he would fit into this picture. What would he talk about with her parents? How would he react to Aria's painting? What would it be like to leave there together as a family and spend the night in his arms?

The fantasy made her suck in a breath. She wanted the fantasy, or at least parts of it. She wasn't ready to get remarried, but she didn't want to give up on her and Wesley. She hoped he came to his senses soon because she'd meant what she'd said. If he didn't realize her feelings were about him and not his status, then her fantasy would be nothing more than that.

Chapter Twenty-Four

Wesley met Tyrone that weekend at the family home to cut the grass and trim the weeds. They knocked everything out in no time and once they finished the two sat on the steps on the front porch with cold beers. The sound of someone else cutting grass down the street along with birds and children playing filled the air.

Tyrone took a deep breath of the warm, humid air and sipped the beer. "Maybe I'll move into the house."

Wesley blinked and turned toward his brother. "What house?"

"This house. To help take care of it. What do you think?"

"I don't know. I thought you were going to move to Atlanta or somewhere."

Tyrone took a sip of his beer. "I thought about it. I'm not saying I'll move in tomorrow or anything, but the thought of it not being here upset me."

"I wasn't trying to upset y'all."

Tyrone nodded. "I know. I'm not saying that. I

understand why you thought about selling. Honestly, if I were in your place, I would probably do the same. But I like having a home base to return to."

"What about your place?"

"You know I'm renting that house. It doesn't have the same feel. I think I'd like to come back here instead." He glanced at Wesley. "Would you mind?"

"You moving in here? Nah, I don't plan to move here."

"You're going to stay in your condo forever?"

Wesley shrugged. "Not forever. I don't want to buy a house unless I've got a reason for all that space."

"What's a reason?"

"You know. Wife, kids, all that. If I ever decide to get married and settle down, then I'll pick a house with her."

Tyrone's eyes narrowed. "Is Cierra 'her'?"

Wesley sighed and leaned back against the column on the porch. "I don't know." He hadn't called her this week because he didn't know what to say. Weak, he knew it, but he didn't feel wrong for questioning her. Yet at the same time he hated that the insecurity he'd felt as a teen was coming back.

"What's that sigh about? You two broke up?"

"Nothing like that. Just a disagreement."

"Who messed up? You or her?"

Wesley thought about their interaction. "This is maybe on me more than her."

"Ah, so now you've got to do some begging," Tyrone said with a grin.

"I've gotta do something," he agreed.

"Just make sure she's the right person," Tyrone said before leaning back on one hand and raising his beer to his lips with the other.

"You're not still on that Cierra-is-trying-to-use-me thing?"

As soon as the words were out of his mouth, he felt like a hypocrite for questioning his brother. He'd basically implied the same thing when he'd confronted her over what her mother had said in the store. Right after she kicked him out, he realized he'd approached the situation incorrectly. He was going to have a hard enough time untangling himself from the misunderstanding. He might as well start with preventing his family from getting caught up in it as well.

Tyrone shook his head. "Not after we talked. From what I remember of Cierra she wasn't manipulative like that."

"So why did you automatically assume she was behind it?"

"It's been different out here dating since the show announcement and everything."

"Different how?"

"More drama."

Wesley gave his brother a side-eye. "Tyrone, you had drama before all of this. Remember the whole deal with Lil Bit and your slashed tires?"

Tyrone shook his head. "I remember. The thing is, that was something that happened here a while ago. But I had this woman I hooked up with in Miami mention it."

Wesley spilled the beer he'd taken a sip of. "How she know?" He wiped his mouth.

Tyrone threw up a hand. "That's what I'm trying to figure out. She said it all sly-like, too. Had me wondering if someone's trying to get me caught up in something."

"Nah, I don't think anyone would do that."

"I don't know. I never worried about my past dating life, but I don't want my past to mess up everything we've worked for. We finally got a show. I want to keep it."

"Don't worry about it. You've dated a lot, but outside of that misunderstanding with Lil Bit you haven't really dogged anyone out." He raised a brow. "Have you?"

Tyrone shook his head. "I haven't. I remember what Dad told us about respecting women. I'm upfront about everything."

"Then we don't have anything to worry about. Just take the same advice you gave me. Be careful out there."

Tyrone nodded and sipped his beer. "I will.

Maybe I should find someone to settle down with like you're doing. Then no one would have anything to say."

Wesley chuckled. "I'm not settled yet. I've got to do a little groveling, remember?"

Chapter Twenty-Five

"You look pretty, Mommy," Aria said from where she sat on Cierra's bed.

Cierra turned away from the full-length mirror to smile at her daughter. "You think so?"

Aria nodded and gave Cierra a thumbs-up. Cierra turned back to the mirror and ran her hands over her dress. She'd pulled a dark orange maxi-style dress with a halter top that gathered at the waist from her closet. The dress was simple, flattering and had never been worn. She'd accessorized with dangling gold earrings and a gold bangle on her wrist.

"Well, I guess I'm ready."

"I wish I could go," Aria said, pouting.

Cierra crossed the room and kissed her daughter's forehead. "I know you do, but Grandma is putting this together for adults. Believe me, you'll have plenty of chances to dress up and go to parties later. Plus, you're going to have a lot of fun with Jaden."

Aria's face lit up at the name of her babysitter. "She said she would bring her art book over the next time."

"Then you'll probably have a lot more fun than I will tonight."

The doorbell rang and Aria jumped up on the bed. "It's Jaden!"

"Let's go see." She took Aria's hand and helped her step down from the bed before they left her bedroom.

She went to the door expecting to find Jaden but was stunned to discover Wesley instead. He was dressed in a dark gray suit, with a white shirt and patterned blue tie. The entire outfit was enough to take her breath away, but what made her heart truly flip was the cake in his hands.

She hadn't called him after kicking him out the other day. They'd never discussed going to the prom together, so she hadn't expected to see him. She really hadn't expected him to show up. Seeing him there, looking as delicious as the cake with an apologetic smile on his face, made her want to haul him inside by the tie, pull him into her arms and forget the rest of the night.

"Mr. Wesley!" Aria exclaimed.

Cierra blinked. "You baked?"

He nodded and came into the house as she stepped back to let him inside. "Hey, Aria," he said then looked at Cierra. "You said your favorite cake is pineapple upside down. I figured if I'm going to apologize I might as well do it right."

Cierra's heart flipped and not just from his words. The fact that he'd shown up and admitted to wanting to apologize opened her up to so many emotions. For years she'd dealt with Troy, who refused to apologize for anything. He always had an excuse for why he did something and often tried to make her feel bad for something he'd done wrong. She'd almost expected the same thing from Wesley.

"You're doing pretty good," Cierra said.

Aria rose onto her toes to try to get a better look at the cake. "Can I have a piece?"

Wesley smiled at her. "That's up to your mom."

Cierra nodded. "One piece tonight."

Aria clapped and reached for the cake. Wesley raised a brow at Cierra, who nodded. He gave the cake to Aria, who immediately hurried farther into the house. Cierra moved to follow but he placed a hand on her elbow. When she faced him, he pulled her into his arms. His eyes were deep and sincere.

"I'm sorry. I shouldn't have accused you of using me."

"I understand why you did. My mom apologizes, too. She was excited and got carried away. She just wants me to be happy."

"That's all I want for you, too, Cierra." He raised his hand to brush his fingers across her cheek. "I just want to make you happy. If my newfound celebrity status helps you in any way, then I'm okay with that."

"But that's not why I'm with you."

"I know that. I was insecure and let that show. That's why I'm right here willing to talk things out. I want this to continue to grow between us. I hope you feel the same."

"I'm not ready to get remarried. Not just yet." Despite what her mom and Aria had said, she had to be up-front with him.

"Did I ask you to marry me?" he said with a raised brow. "We'll worry about that when I do ask. But understand, Cierra, the way I'm feeling, one day I think I just may ask."

Her heart stuttered and she held back a grin. "I may be okay with that…one day."

He lowered his head and his lips brushed hers. She leaned in to deepen the kiss when the sound of a clearing throat interrupted them. Cierra and Wesley both jumped and turned toward the door. Jaden, her babysitter, waved.

"Um…hey, Ms. Cierra. My bad. I didn't mean to interrupt."

"It's okay, Jaden. Aria is in the kitchen. We were just getting ready to leave."

Jaden grinned and nodded before going past them with a twinkle in her eye. Cierra pointed in that direction. "Let me get them settled and then we can go."

Wesley leaned forward and kissed her quickly. "I'll wait right here."

* * *

Wesley could barely stop himself from grinning from ear to ear as he walked into the prom with the most beautiful woman in town on his arm. He didn't care that this was over a decade after the time he was originally supposed to take Cierra to the prom. What happened between them in the past didn't mean he couldn't look forward to a bright future with the woman he loved.

His chest constricted and he sucked in a breath. Love. Damn.

He hadn't expected for that word to pop up so easily. He glanced down at Cierra standing next to him. Her focus was on the crowded ballroom. She smiled and waved at people who called out to her. When she glanced back at him, and her face softened with emotion, the love that surprised him a moment before spread like a warm glow through his system.

Yeah, he loved this woman. He wasn't ashamed or regretful of anyone finding out about his feelings.

"You okay?" she asked.

"I'm wonderful," he said honestly.

"Good, because it looks like everyone who's anyone is here tonight."

"That's good for your mom and the Literacy Council, right?"

She nodded. "Yeah, but it also means everyone is going to be in our business and will want a piece of you."

He shrugged. "I'll be okay. I've got you beside me."

Her eyes softened and he couldn't help himself. He leaned down and kissed her quickly.

"Oh good, you're here," Cierra's mom interrupted. "I need you both to help oversee the silent auction. Come on."

Without another word she pulled them in that direction. Minutes later, his dreams of spending the night dancing with Cierra were dashed as Olivia put them to work. He didn't mind because being occupied kept a lot of people from cornering him and asking questions about his brothers and their new show. He could use the auction or some task assigned by Cierra's mom to escape.

He kept his eyes on Cierra during the night. She was radiant in the orange dress. He wasn't sure when her babysitter was leaving, but he really hoped he got the opportunity to peel the dress off her and kiss every inch of her body. He wasn't the only one who noticed how good Cierra looked. He caught other people giving Cierra appraising glances, including her ex-husband, Troy.

Troy managed to find a reason to be in whatever area Cierra was in all night. Wesley could see her getting increasingly irritated by his unwanted attention. He was debating stepping in and telling Troy to back down when Cierra loudly told the man to leave her alone. The group of people near them looked away and chuckled. Cierra immediately turned her back on Troy and walked away. Troy looked Wesley's way. Wesley didn't bother to hide his grin before turning his back on Troy to do something else.

A few minutes later someone tapped his shoulder. Wesley turned around and was surprised to find Troy.

"You got a second? I need to holla at you," Troy said.

Wesley suppressed a sigh but nodded. "Yeah." He turned to one of the volunteers keeping track of the silent auction. "I'll be right back." The woman nodded and Wesley followed Troy out of the ballroom.

"What's up, Troy?"

Troy turned to him and crossed his arms. "You know she's only seeing you to make me jealous."

Wesley didn't bother to hide his sigh. He pressed a hand to his temple before focusing on Troy. "That's what you brought me out here for?"

"Everyone knows she's only dating you because you got that show. That and she knows it'll get to me."

"Aight, man, if that's what you want to believe." He turned to walk away.

Troy hurried to block his path. "It's not what I want to believe. It's the truth. It's just like high school. She's using you to get to me. I'm just trying to look out for you. For old times' sake."

Wesley stepped forward until only a few inches separated him from Troy. Troy's eyes widened and he leaned back. Wesley didn't smile and made sure his voice was dead serious. "Look, Troy, that messy manipulative stuff you're trying to pull may have worked when I was seventeen, but I'm a grown man now. Whatever you say means nothing. I go by what Cierra has to say. And she's made it very clear that she doesn't want you."

"She's playing hard to get."

"No, she doesn't want you. I've stayed out of it because I realize you're her ex-husband and y'all have Aria. I'm never going to try and step in between your relationship with your daughter, but you need to understand this and understand it quickly. As long as I'm Cierra's man, I won't sit back and watch you press up on her. Grow the hell up and accept that you had your chance and it's over."

"I had her first," Troy said, sounding as pathetic as the words he'd tossed out.

Wesley shrugged. "And? What? I'm supposed to care about that? You really are insecure. Man, get help working that out. Just know, you mess with Cierra and you'll have me to deal with." Wesley eyed him up and down, saw nothing but a weak, wretched version of the confident and charismatic guy he'd once considered a friend and shook his head.

He didn't say anything else as he turned and walked away from Troy.

Chapter Twenty-Six

Cierra nearly panicked as she watched Wesley leave the ballroom with Troy. It took longer than she liked to disentangle herself from a conversation with one of her mom's friends to follow them out. She didn't think they'd fight. They were adults and fighting was off the table, right? But she also didn't put it past Troy to say something dumb and petty enough to get a rise out of Wesley. Or to intentionally try to manipulate the situation.

She was rounding the corner to where they were when their voices carried. She listened as Wesley deflected each one of Troy's weak attempts to undermine their relationship. To hear him defend her while simultaneously break down how pathetic Troy's behavior was made her heart soar.

In that moment she knew she'd gone from potentially falling for Wesley to falling in love with him. His quiet strength and maturity still attracted her to this day.

"Understand, Cierra, the way I'm feeling, one day I think I just may ask." The memory of his

words from earlier made her heart ache with joy. For the first time in a long time the idea of one day getting married again didn't fill her with dread.

"Cierra, do you have a moment?"

Cierra jumped and spun around. She'd been caught eavesdropping, and her face flamed with embarrassment. The woman who spoke, Leslie Bryant, was an older Black woman with short gray hair, dark eyes and a confident stance. She wore a black sequin dress and moderate heels. Cierra recognized her from her position on the town council.

"Yes." She glanced in the direction of where Troy and Wesley talked before directing Leslie away from the men. "What can I help you with?"

"I heard that you're getting the DeWalt Manor turned over to the historical society. Is that true?"

Cierra nodded. She'd met with the head of the historical society and brought up the idea. They'd been thrilled with the idea of trying to take over ownership of the property. It was a big piece of their town's history and they wanted to preserve it.

"I did, but the details aren't worked out yet."

"You may not know it, but the historical society is funded by the town. When they let us know that this was going to be preserved, along with the reason why, I was impressed. You could have made a lot more money selling the place."

"I know, but once I learned the full history I didn't feel right profiting off the pain that property holds. Carolyn DeWalt felt the same way. It's for the best."

"I agree." Sadness filled Leslie's face. "You see, my mom knew Lou Earl Tribble."

Cierra sucked in a breath. "She did?"

Leslie nodded slowly. "When I was younger, she told me about how he'd come by the house to help out her mom. He was sweet on my mom, and she liked him, too. My mom and everyone who knew him were certain he didn't murder that girl. My mom also said Pearly Mae wouldn't just abandon him like that. Knowing that you got to the truth and proved what my family always believed...it goes a long way."

Cierra took Leslie's hand in hers. "I wish I could do more."

Leslie patted her hand. "You did more than enough. I've reached out to the people still alive who remember Lou Earl and Pearly Mae. We're going to try and get the case revisited. We may not have been able to save his life, but maybe we can clear his name."

Cierra had to blink several times to stop the burn of tears from spilling. The idea of clearing Lou Earl's name and bringing peace to his mother's spirit filled her with an immense sense of joy and hope. "I truly hope you can."

Leslie wiped her own eyes and smiled. "It's hard to find someone who has integrity like that. Especially when it comes to money. I'm in the process of selling my current home. I was going to go with Huger Realty, but I'd rather work with you. Can we meet on Monday to discuss the details?"

"O-of course," Cierra stuttered, stunned by the turn of the conversation. "I'd love to help you out."

Leslie nodded and squeezed her hand. "Good. I have a friend looking for a Realtor as well. She lives in Sunshine Beach. Would you be willing to help her?"

"Yes. If you or anyone you know needs a Realtor, send them my way."

"I'll do that. Thanks, Cierra."

Cierra grinned as she watched Leslie walk away. She had another client. Maybe two. She did a quick shimmy. Maybe things would turn around for her.

Large hands clasped her waist before Wesley's amused voice spoke close to her ear. "Hey, girl, don't be shaking like that."

Cierra grinned and looked at him over her shoulder. "Why not?"

His eyes sparked with a delicious devilment. "Because it's giving me ideas."

Cierra leaned back and lowered her voice. "What kind of ideas?"

"Ideas like skip the rest of this prom, go back to my place and strip you out of this dress."

Her body immediately heated. "Don't play with me like that."

He raised a brow. "Who says I'm playing?"

"My mom is going to kill us."

He kissed her cheek then whispered, "That's worth the risk."

The heat intensified in her midsection and settled heavily between her thighs. "Let's go."

She sent her mom a quick text saying they had to leave, and they were out. Their clothes were gone the second they crossed Wesley's threshold. She wasn't sure how they made it to the bedroom without falling and breaking something in their rush to be together. She didn't care about the hows when Wesley settled heavily between her thighs and pushed so far and deep she couldn't do anything but cry out in pleasure.

Later, they lay in each other's arms, sweaty and exhausted. As she listened as Wesley's heart slowly returned to a normal beat, she told him about her conversation with Leslie and her plans to have Lou Earl's case reopened.

"Good," he said, the same hope she felt before thick in his voice. "I hope it works out."

"So do I," Cierra said. "Thank you so much for helping me find closure on this."

He ran his hands up and down her back. "I love you," he whispered.

Cierra's head jerked up. "Say what?"

He stared back, his expression calm and serious. "I love you."

A smile spread across her face. "I love you, too."

He let out a breath she assumed he'd been holding, and she leaned up and kissed him. When she leaned back, she grinned. "You know something funny."

"What?"

"Back in high school, this was how I'd hoped prom night would end."

His eyes widened. "Were you planning to seduce me?"

She pressed a hand over her face and laughed. "I didn't know how to seduce. I just knew you always made my body tingle and I wanted you to touch it everywhere."

Wesley slowly eased her hand from her face. "You have no idea how much I wanted to touch you everywhere back then."

"Too bad it took this long."

He shook his head. "Not too bad at all. Because now, I plan to touch, kiss and love you hopefully for the rest of my life."

Cierra rolled over onto her back and tugged him along with her until his body blanketed hers. "I can get down with that," she said before pulling his head down and kissing him again.

* * * * *

*Don't miss the next book in the
Heart & Soul miniseries,*

Counterfeit Courtship

*Coming December 2022 from
Harlequin Special Edition!*

#2935 THE MAVERICK'S MARRIAGE PACT
Montana Mavericks: Brothers & Broncos • by Stella Bagwell

To win an inheritance, Maddox John needs to get married as quickly as possible. But can he find a woman to marry him for all the wrong reasons?

#2936 THE RIVALS OF CASPER ROAD
Garnet Run • by Roan Parrish

When heartbroken Bram Larkspur finds out the street he's just moved onto has a Halloween decorating contest, he thinks it's a great way to meet people. He isn't expecting to meet Zachary Glass, the buttoned-up architect across the street who resents having competition...and whom he's quickly falling for.

#2937 LONDON CALLING
The Friendship Chronicles • by Darby Baham

Robin Johnson has just moved to London after successfully campaigning for a promotion at her job and is in search of a new adventure and love. After several misfires, she finally meets a guy she is attracted to and feels safe with, but can she really give him a chance?

#2938 THE COWGIRL AND THE COUNTRY M.D.
Top Dog Dude Ranch • by Catherine Mann

Dr. Nolan Barnett just gained custody of his two orphaned grandchildren and takes them to the Top Dog Dude Ranch to bond, only to be distracted by the pretty stable manager. Eliza Hubbard just landed her dream job and must focus. However, they soon find the four of them together feels a lot like a family.

#2939 THE MARINE'S CHRISTMAS WISH
The Brands of Montana • by Joanna Sims

Marine captain Noah Brand is temporarily on leave to figure out if his missing ex-girlfriend's daughter is his—and he needs his best friend Shayna Wade's help. Will this Christmas open his eyes to the woman who's been there this whole time?

#2940 HER GOOD-LUCK CHARM
Lucky Stars • by Elizabeth Bevarly

Rory's amnesia makes her reluctant to get close to anyone, including sexy neighbor Felix. But when it becomes clear he's the key to her memory recovery, they have no choice but to stick very close together.

He opened the mailbox absently and reached inside. There should be an issue of *Global Architecture*. But the moment the mailbox opened, something hit him in the face. Shocked, he reeled backward. Had a bomb gone off? Had the world finally ended?

He sputtered and opened his eyes. His mailbox, the ground around it and presumably he himself were covered in...glitter?

"What the...?"

"Game on," said a voice over his shoulder, and Zachary turned to see Bram standing there, grinning.

"You— I— Did you—?"

"You started it," Bram said, nodding toward the dragon. "But now it's on."

Zachary goggled. Bram had seen him. He'd seen him do something mean-spirited and awful, and had seen it in the context of a prank… He was either very generous or very deluded. And for some reason, Zachary found himself hoping it was the former.

"I'm very, very sorry about the paint. I honestly don't know what possessed me. That is, I wasn't actually possessed. I take responsibility for my actions. Just, I didn't actually think I was going to do it until I did, and then, uh, it was too late. Because I'd done it."

"Yeah, that's usually how that works," Bram agreed. But he still didn't seem angry. He seemed…impish.

"Are you…enjoying this?"

Bram just raised his eyebrows and winked. "Consider us even. For now." Then he took a magazine from his back pocket and handed it to Zachary. *Global Architecture.*

"Thanks."

Bram smiled mysteriously and said, "You never know what I might do next." Then he sauntered back across the street, leaving Zachary a mess of uncertainty and glitter.

Don't miss
The Rivals of Casper Road by Roan Parrish,
available October 2022 wherever
Harlequin Special Edition books and ebooks are sold.

Harlequin.com

HSEEXP0822

HARLEQUIN
PLUS

Announcing a **BRAND-NEW** multimedia subscription service for romance fans like you!

Read, Watch and Play.

Experience the easiest way to get the romance content you crave.

HARLEQUIN

Heartfelt or thrilling, passionate or uplifting—Harlequin is more than just happily-ever-after.

With twelve different series to choose from and new books available every month, you are sure to find stories that will move you, uplift you, inspire and delight you.